I could get used to being with this woman, Aaron thought as he watched Allison lean her head back and close her eyes.

Can I really set my fears about marriage aside and try to build a relationship with her? I want to. In fact, I've never wanted anything so much or felt so happy as when I'm with her. He grimaced. *But she'll be leaving for Pennsylvania in a few months, and then what?*

Aaron cleared his throat, and Allison's eyes popped open. "What's wrong? Have you got a nibble?" she asked, glancing at the end of his pole.

"Nope. I just wanted to ask you something."

"What is it?"

"I was wondering. . ." Aaron fought the temptation to bite off a fingernail. Why did he feel so tongue-tied, when all he wanted to do was ask her a simple question?

"What were you wondering?" she prompted.

He drew in a deep breath, hoping it would give him the courage to say what was on his mind. "I enjoy your company and would like to court you, Allison. I was hopin' you might consider staying on here longer instead of leaving in August like you'd planned."

Allison smiled at Aaron so sweetly he knew he had to kiss her right then.

He leaned toward Allison; his lips were inches from hers. The boat began to vibrate. He tried to steady it, but there wasn't time. In one quick movement, the canoe rolled over, and *splash*—they were plunged into the chilly water.

WANDA E. BRUNSTETTER lives in central Washington with her husband Richard who is a pastor. She has two grown children and six grandchildren. Wanda is a professional ventriloquist and puppeteer and has done programs for children of all ages. Wanda's greatest joy as an author is writing about the Amish, whose simple lifestyle and commitment to God and family are a reminder of something we all need. Wanda invites you to visit her Web site: www.wandabrunstetter.com.

Books by Wanda E. Brunstetter

HEARTSONG PRESENTS

HP254—A Merry Heart
HP421—Looking for a Miracle
HP465—Talking for Two
HP478—Plain and Fancy
HP486—The Hope Chest
HP517—The Neighborly Thing
HP542—Clowning Around
HP579—Kelly's Chance
HP610—Going Home
HP646—On Her Own
HP662—Dear to Me

Don't miss out on any of our super romances. Write to us at the following address for information on our newest releases and club information.

Heartsong Presents Readers' Service
PO Box 721
Uhrichsville, OH 44683

Or visit www.heartsongpresents.com

Allison's Journey

Wanda E. Brunstetter

Heartsong Presents

To my good friend, Leeann Curtis, who makes beautiful Amish dolls (www.facelessfriends.com). And to my aunt, Elma Thompson, who helped me know Jesus when I was a young girl.

A note from the Author:
I love to hear from my readers! You may correspond with me by writing:

Wanda E. Brunstetter
Author Relations
PO Box 721
Uhrichsville, OH 44683

ISBN 1-59310-786-2

ALLISON'S JOURNEY

Our mission is to publish and distribute inspirational products offering exceptional value and biblical encouragement to the masses.

All of the characters and events in this book are fictitious. Any resemblance to actual persons, living or dead, or to actual events is purely coincidental.

All scripture quotations, unless otherwise noted, are taken from the King James Version of the Bible.

PRINTED IN THE U.S.A.

one

Allison Troyer stepped into the kitchen, prepared to help her aunt fix breakfast. Today was Allison's nineteenth birthday, but she was sure Aunt Catherine wouldn't make a fuss over it. In the twelve years Papa's *eldi maedel*—old maid—sister had been living with them, she'd never made much over Allison's or any of her five older brothers' birthdays. Allison figured her aunt didn't care for children and had only moved from her home in Charm, Ohio, to Bird-in-Hand, Pennsylvania, because she felt a sense of obligation to Allison's father, her brother. After Mama's untimely death, Papa had been left to raise six children, and it would have been difficult for him without his sister's help.

Allison glanced at her aunt, standing in front of their propane-operated stove. She was a tall, large-boned woman with big hands and feet. Aunt Catherine's gray-streaked, mousy brown hair was done up tightly in a bun at the back of her head, her stiff, white *kapp* set neatly on top.

The wooden floor creaked as Allison stepped across it, and her aunt whirled around. Her skin looked paler than normal this morning, making her deeply set blue eyes seem more pronounced.

"*Gude mariye,*" Allison said.

"Mornin'," Aunt Catherine replied, her thin lips set in a firm line. "You want your eggs fried or scrambled?"

"Whatever seems easiest."

"It's your birthday, so you choose."

Allison smiled. So Aunt Catherine hadn't forgotten. Maybe this year she would bake Allison a cake. "I prefer scrambled. Would you like me to set the table or make some toast?"

"I think it would be best if you set the table. Last time you

5

made toast, it was burned on the edges."

If you'd let me do more in the kitchen, I might know how to do things better. Allison gritted her teeth, but without voicing her thoughts, she opened the cupboard door and removed four plates and glasses, placing them on the table.

"Thought I might make a batch of peanut brittle after the chores are done," Aunt Catherine said as she went to the refrigerator and withdrew a jug of milk. "Your brothers and their families will probably join us for supper tonight, and I'm sure some would enjoy the candy."

Allison wrinkled her nose. She liked peanut brittle, but it wasn't as good as moist chocolate cake. Sally Mast, Allison's best friend as well as her brother Peter's girlfriend, always had a cake on her birthday. Of course, Sally's *mamm* was still living and cared about her eight *kinner*. Allison wasn't sure Aunt Catherine cared about anyone but herself.

Allison had just set the last fork in place when Papa and Peter entered the kitchen.

"Hallich gebottsdaag," Papa said, giving Allison a hug.

"Jah," Peter added. "Happy birthday from me, too." He handed her a brown paper sack. "Hope ya like this, sister."

Allison placed the sack on the table, reached inside, and withdrew a baseball glove. She grinned at her blond-haired, blue-eyed brother. "This is just what I needed, Pete. *Danki.*"

Peter smiled and squeezed her arm. "Now you'll be able to play ball a lot easier."

Papa cleared his throat real loud, and Allison and Peter turned to face him. "I've got something for you, too." He handed Allison an envelope, which she quickly tore open. If there was money inside, she planned to buy a new baseball to go with the glove, as her old one was pretty worn.

Allison stared at the piece of paper inside the envelope. "A bus ticket?"

Papa nodded, his brown eyes shining with obvious pleasure. "It's to Seymour, Missouri, where your aunt Mary and uncle Ben King live."

Allison's forehead wrinkled as she studied the ticket and realized she was supposed to leave in two days. Tears welled up in her eyes, and she sank into the closest chair.

"Aren't you happy about this?" her father asked, running his fingers through his thick brown hair. "I figured you'd be excited about making a trip to Missouri."

"I—I had no idea you wanted me to move away," she said with a sniff.

"Oh, Allison," he said kindly as he took a step forward. "I'm not sendin' you there for good. It's just for the summer."

That bit of news gave Allison some relief, but she still didn't understand why her *daed* wanted her to be gone all summer. With the garden coming up, it was Allison's job to keep the weeds down, and it was one of the few chores she actually enjoyed. "Can't I spend the summer right here in Lancaster County?" she asked in a quavering voice.

Papa glanced at Aunt Catherine, like he hoped she might say something, but the woman kept her back to them as she cracked eggs into a glass bowl.

Allison squeezed her eyes shut. *Was this Aunt Catherine's idea? Does she want to get rid of me?*

Papa touched Allison's shoulder, and she opened her eyes. "I thought you might enjoy gettin' to know your *mamm*'s twin sister and her family. Mary's a fine woman who can cook and clean like nobody's business. From the letters she's written, I happen to know that she has a way with the sewin' machine, too."

"Not like me; that's what your daed's saying," Aunt Catherine spoke up. "I've never been able to do much more than basic mending, but maybe that's because. . ." Her voice trailed off, and she started beating the eggs real hard.

Allison looked up at her father. "Are you sending me to Missouri because you think I should learn to cook and sew?"

Papa motioned to the baseball glove lying in Allison's lap. "Thanks to bein' raised with five older brothers, you've become a tomboy. Truth is, you'd rather be outside playin' ball than in the house doin' womanly things."

Peter, who had wandered over to the sink to wash his hands, added his two cents' worth. "Allison always did prefer doin' stuff with the boys. Even when she was little and the girl cousins came around with their dolls, Allison preferred playin' ball or going fishin'."

Allison grunted. "What's wrong with that?"

"If you're ever to find a suitable mate and get married, you'll need to know how to cook, sew, and manage a house well," Papa asserted.

As much as Allison didn't want to leave her home, she didn't wish to seem ungrateful for her daed's birthday surprise. If learning to cook and sew meant she might find a husband, she supposed she had better be willing. She forced her lips to form a smile and said, "Danki, Papa. I'm sure I'll enjoy my time in Missouri."

❧

When the bell above the door to the harness shop jingled, Aaron Zook looked up from the job of cutting strips of leather. His best friend, Gabe Swartz, stepped into the room carrying a broken bridle. "Hey, Aaron, how's business?" He dropped the strap to the workbench.

"Fair to middlin'," Aaron replied. "Business always seems to pick up in the summertime."

Gabe glanced around, his hazel-colored eyes taking in the entire room. "Where's Paul? I figured he'd be up front mindin' the desk while you were in the back room doin' all the work." He chuckled. "Ain't that how it usually is?"

Aaron grimaced. He knew his friend was only funning with him, but the truth was, his stepfather did like to be in charge of the books. Sometimes Aaron felt like he was stuck with the dirty work, the way he'd been when he was a boy helping out in the shop. At least now he was getting paid for it.

"Paul, Mama, and my sisters went to Springfield for the day. Bessie had an appointment with the dentist, and afterward they were plannin' to go over to the sporting goods store so

Paul could see about gettin' a new fishing pole."

Gabe scratched the side of his head, letting his wavy brown hair sift through his fingers. "Where are your brothers? How come they didn't go along?"

"Joseph and Zachary took Davey into Seymour to the farmer's market."

Gabe clucked his tongue. "Which left you here at the shop by yourself all day."

"That's about the size of it. Somebody's gotta keep the place open." Aaron stared wistfully out the window. "I'd much rather be fishing on a sunny morning like this."

"Jah, me, too."

"So how are things at your place?" Aaron questioned. "Has Melinda taken in any new critters lately?"

Gabe grinned. "Almost every week she either finds some animal that's been orphaned or is hurt. Folks are still bringing her wounded animals to care for, too."

Aaron fingered Gabe's broken bridle. "Guess there's never a dull moment in your life, eh?"

"That's for certain sure." Gabe leveled Aaron with a serious look. "When are you gonna settle down and find yourself a nice little gal and get married?"

Aaron's ears burned, and he knew he was the verge of a full-blown blush. "Aw, I ain't ready for marriage."

"Wouldn't you like someone to cuddle and keep you warm on cold nights?"

"Rufus is good at that. He likes to sleep at the foot of my bed."

"*Puh!* No flea-bitten mongrel can take the place of a flesh-and-blood woman." Gabe poked Aaron on the arm. "Besides, think how nice it would be to have someone pretty and sweet to cook, clean, and take care of you 'til you're old and gray."

"Don't need anyone to care for me."

"What about love? Don't ya want to fall in love?"

Aaron stiffened. Why did Gabe keep going on about this? Was he trying to goad him into an argument, or did he think it was fun to watch Aaron's ears turn red?

"I know you're dead set against marriage," Gabe continued, "but if the right woman came along, would you make a move to court her?"

Aaron shrugged. "Maybe, but she'd need to have the same interests as me. She would have to be someone who wasn't afraid of hard work or gettin' her hands dirty."

"You mean like your mamm?"

"Jah. She and my real daed worked well together in the harness shop. She and Paul did, too."

"I wonder if Barbara misses working here now." Gabe motioned to the stack of leather piled on the floor a few feet away. "I heard her tell my mamm once that she actually liked the smell of leather."

Aaron nodded. "I think she does miss it some, but she's got her hands full taking care of Grandpa and Grandma Raber now. Their health is failin', and they seem to need her more all the time."

Gabe nodded soberly. "It must be hard gettin' old and not bein' able to do so much. Can't say as I'm lookin' forward to that in the days ahead."

"Me neither, but there's no point in worryin' about such things now." Aaron picked up the bridle and stroked the broken end. "I love the feel of leather between my fingers, and I'm hopin' to take this shop over someday—when Paul's ready to retire, that is."

"You think that'll be anytime soon?"

Aaron shook his head. "I doubt it. He enjoys workin' here too much."

"Maybe he'll give the shop to you, the way my daed gave the woodworking business to me after Melinda and I got married."

Aaron squinted. "You sayin' I'd have to find a wife and settle down before Paul would be willing to let me take the place over?"

"Not necessarily."

"My real *daed* wanted me to have this business. He told me that more than once before he was killed."

Gabe leaned against the workbench and frowned. "You were pretty young back then. Don't see how you can remember much of anything that was said."

Aaron dropped the bridle, moved over to the desk, and picked up a pen and the work order book. "I was barely nine when Papa's buggy was hit by that truck, but I remember more than you think."

Gabe followed him across the room. "*Ach!* You don't have to get so testy."

Aaron took a seat at the desk. "How soon are you needin' this to be ready?"

"No big hurry. I've got others I can use for now."

"By the end of next week?"

"Sure, that'll be fine." Gabe moved away from the desk. "Guess I should be gettin' back home. Melinda and I are planning to go to Seymour later today. We want to see if the owner of the bed-and-breakfast needs more of her drawings or my handcrafted wooden items for his gift shop."

"Okay. See you Sunday morning at preaching. It's to be held at the Kings' place this time around, ain't that so?"

"Yep." Gabe started for the door. "Maybe we can get a game of baseball going after the common meal," he called over his shoulder.

Aaron smiled. "I hope so."

The door clicked shut behind Gabe, and Aaron headed to the back room. He had some leather strips that needed to be dyed and, after that, there was a saddle to clean. Maybe if he finished up early today there would be time enough to get in a little fishing. At least that was something to look forward to—that and a good game of baseball on Sunday afternoon.

two

Allison stared out the window at the passing scenery as the bus took her farther from home and all that was familiar. She would be gone three whole months, living with strangers in a part of the country she'd never seen before—because Papa thought she needed to learn to be more feminine. Maybe by the time she returned to Pennsylvania, she would be ready for marriage. Of course she would need to fall in love with someone first.

Allison glanced at the canvas bag by her feet. Inside was the book she'd brought along to read, as well as some of Aunt Catherine's peanut brittle—a gift for Aunt Mary's family. Allison's faceless doll was also in the bag. It had been in her possession since she was a little girl. Papa said Mama had made it, but Allison didn't remember receiving the doll. In fact, all memories of her mamm were vague. She'd only been seven when Mama died, and Papa had said a car hit his unsuspecting wife's buggy when she'd pulled out of their driveway. Allison had supposedly witnessed the accident, but she had no memory of it. All these years she'd clung to the bedraggled faceless doll, knowing it was her only link to the mother she'd barely known. She'd named the doll Martha, after Mama.

Allison reached down and plucked the cloth doll from the canvas satchel. Its arms had come loose long ago and were pinned in place, and its legs hung by a couple of threads. "Mama," she murmured against the small white kapp tied to the doll's head. "Why'd you have to leave me?"

Allison was sure if her mother were still alive, she would have mended the doll. Aunt Catherine probably could have done so, but whenever Allison mentioned it, her aunt said she was too busy to be bothered with something as unimportant as an old doll. *If I could sew better, I would have fixed my little Martha.*

She continued to stare at the doll, realizing that she felt faceless and neglected, like tattered old Martha. Allison's life had no real purpose. She had no goals or plans for the future. She'd spent most of her life trying to stay out of Aunt Catherine's way. *Maybe a few months of separation will be good for both of us. She'll probably be happier with me gone, anyway.*

Allison returned the doll to the satchel and reached for her book about the Oregon Trail. If she kept her mind busy reading, maybe she wouldn't feel so sad.

❧

With a weary sigh, Allison reached for her canvas tote and stood. It had taken a day and a half to get from Lancaster, Pennsylvania, to Springfield, Missouri, by bus. From Springfield, the bus headed for the small town of Seymour, where someone was supposed to pick her up at Lazy Lee's Gas Station. She'd slept some on the bus but hadn't rested nearly as well as she would have in her own bed. Her dark blue cotton dress was wrinkled, and she knew she must look a mess.

Allison made her way down the aisle and stepped off the bus. She spotted a young Amish man with red hair standing beside an open buggy. When he started toward her, she noticed his deeply set blue eyes and face full of freckles.

"I'm your cousin, Harvey King. You must be Allison," he said with a lopsided grin.

She nodded. "Jah, I am."

He motioned to the suitcases being taken from the luggage compartment in the side of the bus. "Show me which one is yours, and I'll put it in the buggy for you."

Allison pointed to a black canvas suitcase, and Harvey hoisted it and her small satchel to the back of his buggy. Then he helped her into the passenger's side, took his place in the driver's seat, and gathered up the reins.

"Mom will be glad to see you," he said as they pulled out of the parking lot. "Ever since your daed phoned and said you were coming, she's been bustlin' around the house gettin' ready for your arrival."

Allison's eyebrows lifted. "You've got a telephone? Is it outside in a shed?"

He shook his head. "No, but they do have one at the harness shop, and from what I was told, your daed and Paul know each other."

She tipped her head. "I didn't realize that."

"He and his stepson Aaron run our local harness shop, but Paul used to live in Lancaster County and worked at a harness shop there."

Allison figured Papa must have either stayed in contact with Paul, or else Abe, the owner of the harness shop near their place, had put him in touch with the man. Papa had obviously phoned Paul's harness shop and left a message for Aunt Mary, letting her know that Allison was coming and what time her bus would get in.

"I hope you don't mind a little detour, but I need to stop by the harness shop before we go home," Harvey said. "I would have done it on my way to Seymour, but I got a late start and didn't want to miss your bus."

"That's okay. I don't mind stopping," Allison assured him. "Fact is, I've been sitting on that bus so long, it'll feel good to get out and move around a bit."

Harvey cast her a sidelong glance. "I figured you'd just wait in the buggy while I run in and pick up my daed's new harness. But if you'd like to go into the shop or walk around outside the place, that's fine by me."

&

"You finished pressing those rivets into that harness yet, Aaron?" Paul called from the front of the shop. "Ben King said his son would be over sometime today to pick it up, and it should have been ready this morning."

Aaron frowned. Why did his stepfather always have to check up on him? Did Paul think he was incapable of getting the job done on time? He clenched his teeth to keep from offering an unkind retort. Truth was, he and Paul did have a fairly good relationship. Ever since that day when Aaron was a boy and Paul had rescued him from the top rung of the silo ladder, they'd been friends. Before that, Aaron had resented the man because he was afraid the man wanted to marry his mamm. Paul had married Mama, and he'd become like a second father to Aaron and his three brothers, even though he tended to be a little bossy at times. Aaron had to wonder if Paul would ever let him take over the harness shop.

"Aaron, did you hear what I said?" Paul called.

"I heard, and the harness is almost done."

"Good, because I looked out the window and saw Harvey pulling up."

Aaron snapped the last rivet into place, picked up the harness, and headed to the front of the shop. He reached Paul's desk in time to see the front door open, and in walked Harvey with a young Amish woman Aaron had never seen before. Her hair was the color of dark chocolate, and she was of medium height and slender build. Had Harvey found himself a new girlfriend? If so, she wasn't from around here; that was for certain sure. Maybe she was from one of the Amish communities up north, near Jamesport.

"Afternoon, Harvey," Paul said with a friendly smile. "You come by for your daed's harness?"

"Jah." Harvey turned to the woman at his side. "This is Allison Troyer. She's my cousin and is here from Pennsylvania for the summer."

Paul took a step forward. "You're Herman's daughter, aren't you?"

"I am." Allison glanced at Aaron and smiled, kind of shylike.

"I took the message when he phoned to say you were coming," Paul said.

How come I didn't know about it? Aaron wondered. *I had no idea Harvey had a cousin living in Pennsylvania.*

Paul took the harness from Aaron. "Here's what you came

for, Harvey. I hope it's done to your daed's liking."

"Looks fine to me."

"Where are my manners? Allison, this is my son, Aaron."

Feeling a bit shy himself, Aaron mumbled, "It's nice to meet you."

She nodded. "Same here."

"Guess I'd better settle up with you and get on home." Harvey moved to the desk. "Mom is probably pacing the floors, waiting for me to show up with her niece."

As Paul wrote out the invoice and Harvey leaned on the desk, Aaron ambled over to one of their workbenches and picked up a piece of leather that needed to be cut and dyed. He was surprised when Allison followed.

"Sure smells nice in here," she said, tilting her head and sniffing the air.

"You really think so?"

"I do."

"Most women don't care much for the smells inside a harness shop. Except for my mamm, that is," Aaron corrected. "She used to work here with my real daed, and then she took the place over by herself for a time after he died. When she and Paul married, Mama kept workin' in the shop, but after my grandparents' health began to fail, she gave it up in order to see to their needs."

Allison stared at Aaron, and his ears began to burn. He didn't know what had made him blab all that information to a woman he'd only met.

"I can see why your mamm would enjoy working here," Allison said, motioning to the pile of leather on the floor. "This looks like a fun place to be."

Aaron was about to comment when Harvey sauntered up, holding the finished harness. "Guess we'd better get going," he said, nodding at Allison.

She gave Aaron a quick smile. "Maybe I'll see you again sometime."

"No maybe about it. You'll see him at church tomorrow

mornin'." Harvey winked at Aaron, but before he could think of a sensible reply, Harvey and his cousin walked out the door.

≥∂

As Allison and Harvey continued their drive down Highway C, she was amazed at how different the area looked from what she was used to in Pennsylvania. There were no rolling hills, but a multitude of trees, with Amish and English houses built on the land that had been cleared. Most of the homes looked old, and many were run-down. Few had flowers in abundance the way most Amish places did back home. However, the two-story gray and white home that loomed before them as they turned onto a graveled driveway was an exception. A bounty of irises danced in the breeze near the vegetable garden growing to the left of the house, and two pots of pink flowers graced the front porch.

Harvey had no more than guided the horse to the hitching rail when the front door opened and a middle-aged woman followed by a young boy and a girl hurried to the buggy.

When Allison climbed down, the woman gave her a hug. "I'm your aunt Mary, and these are my youngest children, Sarah, who is twelve, and Dan, who's ten."

Allison noticed immediately that Aunt Mary had the same dark hair and brown eyes with little green flecks as she had. Since she barely remembered her mamm, she couldn't be sure her mother's twin sister looked like Mama. But Papa had said they were identical, which meant this was probably how Mama would have looked if she were still alive.

"It's nice to meet you, Aunt Mary." Allison turned to face the children. "You, too, Cousin Sarah and Dan."

"Actually, we have met before," Aunt Mary said. "I came to Pennsylvania for your mamm's funeral."

Allison stared at the ground. "Sorry, but I don't remember that."

"You were quite young then, so I don't expect you would remember." Aunt Mary put her arm around Allison's shoulder. "Should we go inside and have us a glass of lemonade? It's turned into a real scorcher today."

Allison licked her lips, realizing they were parched and that she was rather thirsty. "Jah. That would be nice."

"I'll put the horse away and bring in her suitcase," Harvey said as Allison, Aunt Mary, and her two younger children headed for the house.

"Sounds *gut*, and when you're done, come join us in the kitchen," his mother called over her shoulder.

Allison found herself beginning to relax. *Aunt Mary seems so different from Aunt Catherine. Of course I'd best wait until I get to know her better to make any decisions.*

three

Allison sat around the supper table that evening, amazed at the camaraderie. There were no sharp remarks from Aunt Mary—only smiles and encouraging words. Uncle Ben was kind and friendly, but then Papa and her brothers had always been that way, too. It was Aunt Catherine who made Allison feel as if she could do nothing right. No jokes were tolerated at the table, and the woman often hurried them through their meals, saying there were more chores needing to be done.

Allison had never been able to talk about her feelings with Aunt Catherine, and Papa didn't seem to have much time to listen. Here, everyone seemed interested in what others in the family had to say.

She glanced at Cousin Harvey, who sat beside his fifteen-year-old brother, Walter. The younger teenaged boy had been in the fields with his father when Allison had arrived earlier, so this was the first chance she'd had to meet him. Both Harvey and Walter seemed polite and easygoing, and so did Dan and Sarah.

"Allison brought us some peanut brittle," Aunt Mary said to her husband. "Since it's your favorite candy, I hope you'll let the rest of us have some."

Uncle Ben chuckled, and his crimson beard jiggled up and down. "Jah, sure. I'll share but only a *bissel*."

"Ah, Pop," Walter said with a frown, "don't ya think we deserve more than a little?"

Uncle Ben wiggled his eyebrows playfully. "Well, maybe." Then he glanced over at Allison. "It was nice of your daed's sister to send the peanut brittle. She must be a right thoughtful woman."

Allison almost choked on the piece of chicken she had just

19

put in her mouth. If Uncle Ben knew Aunt Catherine the way she did, he might not think she was so thoughtful.

"Are you all right?" Aunt Mary asked, patting Allison on the back.

"I'm fine. Just choked on a piece of meat." Allison reached for her glass and took a gulp of water.

"I met your aunt Catherine at your mamm's funeral," Aunt Mary said. "You said earlier that you don't remember me being there."

Allison nodded. "I was only seven when Mama died, so I don't remember much of anything during that time."

"Are you saying you don't remember your mamm at all?" Uncle Ben asked.

"I have some memories from before the accident, but they're kind of vague."

"Martha and I were so close when we were growing up," Aunt Mary said wistfully. "It was hard on both of us when I moved to Missouri. We kept in good touch through letters until her passing."

"What made you move to Missouri?" Allison asked.

"That was my fault," Uncle Ben interjected. "I wanted to get away from all the tourists in Lancaster County, and I had a brother who had moved to Missouri. So shortly after Mary and I got married, we caught a bus and headed for Webster County."

Allison wondered if her life would be any different if her Aunt Mary and Uncle Ben still lived in Pennsylvania. There would have been no need for Aunt Catherine to move in with them after Mama's death if Aunt Mary had lived closer. She took another sip of water. *Oh, well. As Papa always says, "Since you can't change the past, you might as well make the best of the present." So I will try to enjoy my summer here.*

৯৯

The following morning before church began, Allison took a seat on the women's side of the room, choosing one end of a bench next to a young, blond-haired woman who looked to be about her age. She glanced around the room and was surprised to see how few people filled the backless benches that had been set up in the Kings' living room. At home there would have been twice as many people in attendance, but then she knew this Amish community was much smaller than hers in Lancaster County.

Allison felt someone touch her arm, and she glanced to the left. The blond-haired woman smiled. "Hi. My name's Katie Esh." Her vivid blue eyes sparkled like ripples of water on a summer day, and Allison noticed a small dimple set in the middle of her chin.

"I'm Allison Troyer, visiting from Pennsylvania."

"How long will you be here?"

"Until the end of August. I'm staying with my aunt and uncle, Mary and Ben King."

Katie leaned closer and whispered in Allison's ear, "Looks like the service is getting ready to start. We can talk later, jah?"

Allison nodded and smiled. It looked like she might have made a friend already.

૨૦

All during the preaching service, Aaron kept glancing at the women's side of the room to see what Allison Troyer was doing. There was something about her that fascinated him. Was it the way she stared longingly out the window, as though she would rather be outdoors? Or was it her chocolate brown hair with curly tendrils that had escaped her kapp and framed her face in such a cute way?

Aaron gripped his hymnbook and tried to focus on the words they were singing, but it was no use. Allison had his full attention. *Maybe it's the fact that she mentioned yesterday how she liked the smell of leather. Since she'll only be here a few months, there won't be much opportunity for me to get to know her.* He frowned. *It's just as well, since I have no plans of courting or settling down to marriage.*

When the service was over, Aaron made his way to the barn, where the common meal would be served. He noticed Allison and Katie pouring coffee for some of the men and found himself wishing it were his table Allison had been asked to serve.

Aaron felt a sharp jab to his ribs, and he glanced at Gabe, who sat beside him. "What are you proddin' me for?"

Gabe snickered. "I've been watchin' you make cow eyes at that new girl, Allison."

"I ain't makin' cow eyes." Aaron bit off the end of a fingernail and flicked it over his shoulder onto the floor.

"Are you ever gonna grow up and quit doin' that?"

"Someday—if I feel like it."

"Maybe fallin' in love would make you give up your crude ways."

Aaron elbowed his friend. "A lot you know, and I ain't crude."

"Jah, well, I know a man with a crush when I see one."

"I don't have no crush. I barely know the woman."

Gabe put his finger in the small of Aaron's back. "Why don't you remedy that by goin' over there and talkin' to her? Or are ya too chicken?"

"I ain't scared of nothin'."

"Prove it."

"All right, I will." Aaron hopped off the bench and strolled across the barn. He stopped a few feet from the table where Allison and Katie were serving. His heart hammered so hard he feared it might break through his chest, and he had to take a couple of deep breaths in order to steady his nerves. He couldn't march right up to Allison and start yammering away. What would he say, and what if she thought he was trying to make a play for her? Then again, he didn't want Gabe to think he was a coward.

He took a step back, bumped a table leg, and almost landed in Bishop Frey's lap.

"Whoa there! What do you think you're doin', boy?" the man asked with a grunt.

"S–s–sorry, Bishop," Aaron stammered. "Didn't realize you were behind me." He glanced around. Everyone in the barn seemed to be staring at him, including Allison.

She probably thinks I'm a dummkopp. *And at the moment, I feel like I am a dunce.* Aaron slunk away, knowing he'd be in for more ribbing from Gabe about his near mishap. A little teasing from his friend would be better than facing Allison and feeling more foolish than he already did. No, he wasn't about to start up a conversation with her now.

ða

Allison watched from the sidelines as a group of young men got a game of baseball going. How she longed to join them, but she was new here, and it might seem too forward if she stepped in and asked to be part of the game. Besides, not thinking she might have a need for it while she was here, she'd left her new baseball glove at home. She doubted that she could play as well without it.

"What are you doing over here?" Katie asked, dropping to her knees on the grass beside Allison. "I figured you'd be up on the porch with some of the women, sipping iced tea."

Allison shook her head. "I'd much rather play baseball than visit, and the next best thing to playing is watching the game."

"You sure you're watching the game and not the cute fellows running around the field getting all sweaty and red in the face?"

Allison felt the heat of a blush as she shook her head, unwilling to admit that she had been watching one particular young man. If she weren't mistaken, he'd been eyeing her, too. In fact, when she and Katie had been serving the men, she'd thought Aaron might be about to say something to her. But then he'd tripped and nearly fallen into the bishop's lap. After that, Aaron had rushed out of the barn.

"Who do you think is the cutest one out there?" Katie prompted.

Allison shrugged. "Don't rightly know."

"I've got my eye on Joseph Zook, but I doubt he even knows I'm alive."

Before Allison could respond, Katie rushed on. "There's going to be a singing tonight at the Kauffmans' place. You think you might be going?"

"I guess that depends on whether Harvey's planning to go or not."

"He usually goes to the singings, so there's a good chance he'll be coming to this one."

Allison opened her mouth to say that she would ask Harvey about going, but the ball *whooshed* toward her, and instinctively she reached up and caught it.

"Wow, that was *wunderbaar!*" her cousin Harvey exclaimed. "Never knew a girl could catch a ball so well. And with one hand, no less."

Allison wondered if she should tell Harvey she was an expert ballplayer or let him think she'd caught it by accident.

"Allison wants to join your baseball game," Katie spoke up. "She told me that she'd rather play ball than visit."

Harvey tipped his head and looked at Allison in a most peculiar way. "Is that true?"

She handed the ball to him and smiled. "I've been playing baseball with my brothers since I was a little girl."

"Well, now, maybe you'd like to be on Aaron Zook's team. He's one player short, and if you don't mind playin' with a bunch of rowdy fellows, we'd be happy to have you."

Allison stood and wiped her damp hands on the sides of her dark green dress. "Are you sure about that?"

He nodded. "Course I am. Come on!"

She hesitated and glanced back at Katie, hoping for her approval.

"Go ahead and play," Katie said. "I'll sit here and cheer you on."

"Okay." Allison followed Harvey across the field until he stopped in front of Aaron. Harvey quickly explained that Allison was going to join the game and since Aaron was a player short she could be on his team.

Aaron's dark eyebrows drew together, and Allison figured he would probably say no. Instead, he gave her a quick nod. "You can play left field."

For the next hour, Allison caught several fly balls, made

three home runs, and chocked up more points for Aaron's team than any of his other players. She took some razzing from a few of the guys, but she thoroughly enjoyed herself.

When the game ended, Allison headed toward Katie, but Aaron stepped in front of her. His face was red and sweaty, and he swiped a grimy hand across his forehead. "You sure play well. Never seen a girl who could catch so many balls as you did."

She grinned up at him. "I've always liked playing ball."

He shuffled his feet in the dirt as he ran his fingers through his damp hair. "Well, guess I should get myself somethin' cold to drink."

"I noticed Katie bringing two glasses from the house, so I'm hoping she has some iced tea waiting for me, too."

Aaron stared at the ground. "Maybe I'll see ya tonight at the singing."

"Jah, maybe so."

four

"I'm glad you were willing to go to the singing tonight," Harvey told Allison as he helped her into his open buggy. "It'll be a good chance for you to get to know some of the other young people."

Allison nodded. "I did get acquainted with Katie Esh today after church, and also some of the boys who were involved in the ball game."

Harvey chuckled. "I still can't get over how well you played. I'll bet Aaron Zook was glad I suggested you be on his team."

Thinking about Aaron caused Allison to smile. She was fascinated with him, even though he did seem kind of shy and a bit rough around the edges.

Don't get any ideas, she told herself. *You'll be going home at the end of summer, so there's no point falling for someone who lives here. Besides, Aaron might have no interest in me at all. Especially now that he's seen what a tomboy I am.*

❧

"Think you might get up the nerve to ask someone to ride home in your buggy tonight?" Aaron's eighteen-year-old brother, Joseph, asked Aaron as the two of them entered the Kauffmans' barn.

Aaron's only reply was a quick shrug.

"If you were to ask someone, who would it be?"

"That's my business, don't ya think?"

Joseph blinked and pulled off his straw hat, revealing a crop of thick blond hair. "Ain't you the testy one tonight. I was only makin' sure you didn't have any ideas about askin' Katie Esh if you could take her home."

Aaron waved his hand, like he was swatting at a fly. "I'm not interested in Katie, so don't worry. You've got the green light to ask her yourself."

Joseph's face turned pink as a sunset. "How'd ya know?"

"It don't take no genius to see that you're smitten with her. You act like a lovesick *hundli* every time she's around."

"I ain't no puppy dog."

"But you are lovesick, right?"

Joseph wrinkled his nose. "If you're not willing to tell me who you might offer a ride home to, then I ain't sayin' how I feel about Katie."

"Suit yourself." Aaron sauntered off toward the refreshment table. A glass of cold lemonade and a couple of cookies might help calm his nerves.

ↄ

Allison stepped into the Kauffmans' barn, and the first person she spotted was Aaron Zook. He stood next to the refreshment table, holding a glass in one hand and a cookie in the other. She was tempted to go over and talk to him, but that would be too forward. Besides, Aaron might have a girlfriend, and she didn't want to do anything that could cause trouble between them if he did.

Glancing around the barn, she discovered Katie sitting on a bale of straw talking to Joseph Zook. Since they both had blond hair, they made a striking pair. Allison remembered Katie had mentioned earlier that she had her eye on Joseph.

Katie motioned Allison to come over, but Allison hesitated until she saw Joseph head over to the refreshment table. A few seconds later, she took a seat on the bale of straw next to Katie.

"I'm glad you came tonight. I always enjoy our singings so much." Katie smiled. "Do you have singings in Lancaster County?"

Allison nodded. "We do."

"Do you have a steady boyfriend back home?"

"No. I've not found anyone who interests me." *And no one's shown an interest in me either*.

Katie sighed. "That was Joseph Zook I was talking to before you came over. He's Aaron's younger brother, in case you didn't know. Joseph asked if I'd like a ride home in his buggy tonight."

"What did you say?"

"I said I'd be willing, of course." Katie poked Allison gently on the arm. "From the way the fellows are watching you, I'd say you might have your pick of whose buggy you get to ride in after the singing."

Allison frowned. "What do you mean? I haven't noticed anyone staring at me."

"That's because they're trying to be sneaky about it. But if you keep your eyes open, you'll see what I mean."

With a quick glance around the room, Allison scanned the faces of the men who were present. Katie was right—one young man was watching her, and it wasn't Aaron Zook. It was someone she hadn't seen today—a man who looked a little older than her. He had shiny black hair that was much longer than any of the other fellows in attendance. When he caught her looking at him, he winked and lifted his hand.

Allison looked away. "Who is that guy leaning against the wall over there?" she asked Katie.

"Where?"

Allison didn't want him to see her pointing, so she nodded with her head and said quietly, "Over there by the back wall. The one with the hair black as coal."

Katie pursed her lips. "Oh, that's James Esh, my cousin. He's kind of wild, but I think he's harmless enough." She leaned closer to Allison. "Was he staring at you?"

Allison moistened her lips with the tip of her tongue. "He winked at me."

Before Katie could respond, Joseph showed up with a plate of cookies and some pretzels, which he handed to Katie.

"That's so nice of you, Joseph. Won't you have a seat?" Katie scooted over, and he plunked down beside her. Then Katie turned to Allison and said, "This is Aaron's younger brother, Joseph."

Joseph nodded. "We met today during the ball game, and I was sure impressed with how well you played."

Allison smiled. "Danki."

"My brother wasn't too happy about being one player short at the beginning of the game, but after you joined in, his team sure did rack up the points."

"I was glad I could play. It was lots of fun."

Just then James showed up, carrying a plate of cookies. "Since we haven't been properly introduced, I thought I'd come over and say hello," he said, reaching one hand out to Allison.

"I'm Allison Troyer."

"And I'm—"

"My pushy cousin, James," Katie cut in.

He scowled at her and his dark brows drew together. "I can speak on my own behalf, thank you very much."

Katie stuck out her tongue, but James ignored her. Instead, he squeezed onto the bale of straw beside Allison and handed her the cookies. "You hungry?"

She smiled and took one with chocolate frosting. "Danki." When she glanced across the room, she noticed Aaron standing in the corner with his arms folded. *I wish it were he instead of James who'd brought me the cookies. I wonder if he thinks I'm interested in James.*

For the next several minutes, Allison, James, Katie, and Joseph visited, until the song leader called out the first song—"Mocking Bird Hill." Several people clapped along, and James kept time to the music by tapping his finger on Allison's arm.

She felt uncomfortable sitting here with him as if they were boyfriend and girlfriend, but she figured it would be rude to ask him to leave. So she put a smile on her face and joined in the singing, the whole time keeping one eye on Aaron, who looked like he might have eaten a sour apple.

When the singing finally ended, Allison felt relief. She needed to get out of the stuffy barn and breathe in some fresh air.

"Hey, where ya goin'?" James called as she headed for the door.

"Outside."

"I'll come with you."

A few minutes later, Allison and James stood under a maple tree, staring up at the moonlit sky. "Sure is pretty tonight," James whispered against her ear.

Her only reply was a quick nod.

"Say, I was wondering if you'd be willing to let me take you home tonight," he said smoothly.

Allison shivered, even though the evening air was quite warm. Should she allow him to escort her back to Aunt Mary's? After all, she'd only met James and didn't know anything about him other than the little bit Katie had shared. Still, if she accepted the ride, it would leave Cousin Harvey free to escort someone home without her tagging along.

"What's your answer, Allison?" James prompted.

"I—I guess it would be okay, but I need to speak with my cousin first to make sure he doesn't mind."

"*Ach!* What business is it of Harvey's who gives you a ride home? You're a grown woman, ain't it so?"

"I can't take off without telling him. He'd probably be worried."

James lifted her chin with his thumb. "Okay, tell him then." He pointed to the buggy parked near the end of the barn. "That's my rig—the one with the fancy silver trim. Meet me over there in ten minutes."

꙳

Aaron stood in the shadows watching James help Allison into his buggy, feeling frustrated and not understanding why. He'd spent most of the evening watching Allison and James as they sat together on a bale of straw. By the time the singing ended, he felt cranky as a cat with a sore paw. He scuffed the toe of his boot in the dirt. *James isn't right for Allison. He's a big flirt and he's way too wild.*

Aaron knew that James Esh had been going through his *rumspringa* since he'd turned sixteen. Yet here he was, twenty-one years old and still running wild. Aaron had been baptized and joined the church by the time he was eighteen, but not so with unruly James. That fellow had a mind of his own, and he liked to show off with his fancy buggy and unmanageable horse whenever he had the chance.

He shouldn't even be using that gelding for a buggy horse, Aaron fumed. *And he sure shouldn't be escorting a woman home in a buggy pulled by that crazy critter.*

When James backed his buggy away from the barn, Aaron caught Allison looking at him. At least he thought she had glanced his way. *Should I wave or call out to her? No, that would be really stupid.*

Aaron slunk back into the shadows and ambled toward his own buggy. *Don't know why I care what Allison does. It ain't none of my business if she's interested in James.*

❧

All the way home Harvey's final words to Allison echoed in her head. *James Esh is a wild one and can't be trusted. I can't stop you from ridin' home in his buggy, but I don't think it's a good idea.*

Allison had chosen to ignore her cousin's warning, not wishing to judge James without getting to know him. After all, it wasn't as if James was asking her to go steady. It was just one ride home in his buggy—and he was the first young man to show her this much interest, so it would have been silly to turn him down.

"You don't talk much, do ya?" James asked, breaking into Allison's thoughts.

She shrugged. "I do when there's something to say."

He chuckled and reached for her hand. "A pretty girl like you don't need to say anything as far as I'm concerned."

She eased her hand away and reached up to tuck a wayward strand of hair back under the dark bonnet she wore over her smaller white kapp. "Your horse is nice," she said, for lack of anything better to say.

"Yep, he's one of the finest. But he can get pretty feisty when he wants to."

"I've ridden bareback a time a two, though never on a spirited horse."

James glanced over at her, and his dark eyebrows drew

together. "I heard you played ball today. Too bad I wasn't there to see that."

"Jah, I did."

"And you like to ride horses?"

She nodded.

"Hmm. Maybe I've finally met my match."

Allison wasn't sure what James meant by his last statement, but she decided it would be best not to ask.

They rode in silence for a while. The only sounds were the steady *clop-clop* of the horse's hooves and an occasional *creak* of a cricket. When they turned onto her aunt and uncle's driveway, James pulled back on the reins. The horse and buggy came to a halt, and he slipped one arm around Allison's shoulders. "I'd like to see you again. Maybe we could go on a picnic sometime. Or I could hire a driver and take you to Springfield where there's a whole lot more to see and do than anyplace around here." He smiled, and the right corner of his mouth made a slight slant.

Allison swallowed hard. She didn't want to hurt James's feeling, but she wasn't sure she wanted to go anywhere with him. "My aunt mentioned last night that she'd be needing some help with her garden this summer, so I'll probably be kept pretty busy."

His crooked smile quickly turned into a frown. "Ah, ya can't be workin' every minute."

"I'll have to see how it goes."

James leaned toward her suddenly and bent his head. Before Allison knew what had happened, his lips touched hers.

She jerked back, feeling like she'd been stung by a wasp. "What'd you do that for?"

He snickered and tickled her under the chin. "Just a friendly way of sayin' I hope to see you again."

Allison didn't answer but hopped down from the buggy and sprinted toward the house without looking back. She heard James laugh, then call to his horse, "Giddyup there, boy!"

She hurried up the driveway and stomped up the stairs. *That was my first kiss, and I didn't even enjoy it.*

five

Allison pulled the Log Cabin quilt up over her bed and straightened the pillows. Next, she picked up her faceless doll to lay it at the foot of the bed. Tears gathered in her eyes as she stroked the small kapp perched on the doll's head. It reminded her of home.

After the pleasant welcome she'd received on Saturday, Allison had thought she might do okay here. But even so, she missed Papa and Peter something awful.

She thought about last night and how James Esh had brought her home from the singing and then stolen a kiss. She wondered if he would ask her out again, and if he did, how could she graciously decline?

Allison placed the doll on the bed, moved over to the dresser, and reached for her hairbrush, needing to focus on something else. A vision of Aaron flashed into her mind— dark hair, dark eyes, square jaw, and a smile that made her insides do funny things. He seemed shy compared to James, and he sure hadn't flirted with her the way James had.

Aaron's probably not interested in me because I'm not feminine enough. But then I wonder why James showed an interest.

A knock on the bedroom door drove Allison's thoughts aside. "Come in," she called.

The door opened and Aunt Mary stepped into the room. "I was wondering if you were up."

"I was just getting my hair done." Allison made a part down the middle and rolled her long hair back on the sides, then secured it into a bun.

"Did you have fun at the singing last night?" her aunt asked.

"It was okay. A bit different from the singings we have back home." Allison chose not to mention that James had brought

33

her home or say anything about what had happened before she'd come into the house. She'd been relieved to discover that everyone had gone to bed, for she was certain her flushed cheeks would have let them know something was amiss.

"I'm sure we do many things differently here." Aunt Mary moved over to the bed and picked up Allison's doll. "Looks like this poor thing is in need of repair."

Allison set her kapp in place. "Papa told me that Mama made it for me when I was little, but I don't remember. I've kept it because it's all I have to remind myself that I ever had a mamm."

"I'm sorry about that." Aunt Mary took a seat on the edge of the bed and placed the doll in her lap. "How come her arms are pinned on and her legs are dangling by a few pieces of thread?"

"I don't know how to fix it," Allison said with a sigh. "Several times I've asked Aunt Catherine to repair the doll, but she always said she didn't have the time."

Allison's aunt looked at her in a most peculiar way. "Are you saying no one has ever taught you to sew?"

Allison pointed to the doll. "Whenever I try to sew, I usually manage to stick myself with the needle, and the thread never seems to hold."

"Most women your age know how to sew well. Would you like to learn to use my treadle machine?"

Allison nibbled on the inside of her cheek. Truth be told, she'd never really had a desire to sew.

"We could begin by repairing your faceless doll. Then later, when we have more time, I'd be happy to show you how to make a doll from scratch."

"Well, I—"

"I haven't made a faceless doll for some time, but I think it would be fun," her aunt rushed on. "You might even want to sell some dolls at the farmer's market or in one of the gift shops in Seymour."

The thought of making some money of her own while

she was visiting appealed to Allison, but she wasn't sure she wanted to learn how to sew in order to accomplish that. *Of course,* she reminded herself, *the reason Papa sent me here is so I can learn to do more womanly things. And if I'm ever to find a husband, I'll need to know how to sew, whether I like it or not.*

"Jah, okay. I'd be happy if you could show me how to use the sewing machine," she finally consented.

&

Aaron had just finished his chores in the barn and was about to head to the harness shop when he spotted his collie crouched in the weeds near the garden. "Must have a mouse or some other critter cornered," he muttered.

He moved closer to the dog and soon discovered what Rufus had between his paws was a kitten, not a mouse. "Bad dog! Come here and leave that poor animal alone!"

The collie hesitated, released a pathetic whimper, and then backed slowly away. Aaron figured the cat would take off like a flash, but it just lay there, still as could be.

"Rufus, if you killed Bessie's kitten she'll have your hide. Mine, too, for lettin' you run free." Aaron squatted in front of the ball of gray fur and was relieved to see that it was still breathing. He gently picked it up, checking it over for teeth marks. It didn't appear as if Rufus had bitten the kitten, just scared it real bad. If he put it back in the hayloft with its mother, it should be fine.

Aaron returned to the barn, where he placed the cat with its mother and four other kittens; then he went to find Rufus so he could tie him up for the day.

Several minutes later, Aaron entered the harness shop and found Paul at his workbench assembling an enormous leather harness, which would no doubt be used on a Belgian draft horse.

"How come you're late?" Paul asked.

"I caught Rufus with one of Bessie's kittens, and I knew if I didn't get the critter away from him quickly it would soon be dead."

"You'd better keep the dog tied. Leastways 'til the kittens are big enough to fend for themselves."

"He's chained up now."

"That's *gut*, because your little sister would have a conniption if something happened to one of her cats." Paul motioned to a tub sitting off to one side. "Better get started cleaning and oiling James Esh's saddle. He dropped it by Friday afternoon while you were up at the house getting our lunches."

Just the mention of James's name set Aaron's teeth on edge. He didn't like the way that fellow had looked at Allison last night at the singing, and he especially didn't care for the fact that he'd seen the two of them drive away in James's buggy. *Sure hope he didn't try anything funny with Allison. He's got a reputation for being more than a flirt. If only I'd had the nerve to ask her about a ride myself.*

Aaron's nails bit into his skin as he balled his fingers into tight fists and held his arms stiffly at his side. *What am I thinking? I'm not interested in a relationship with Allison. Courting leads to marriage, and marriage leads to—*

"Aaron, did ya hear what I said?"

Aaron whirled around. "Huh?"

Paul pointed to the tub. "The saddle needs to be cleaned."

"*Jah*, okay. I'll see that it gets done." Aaron set right to work, but he knew it would be hard to concentrate. Ever since last night, his thoughts had been occupied with Allison Troyer and how he wished he could get to know her better.

He shook his head in an attempt to get himself thinking straight. For a long time he'd been telling his friend Gabe that he never planned to get married, so why was he thinking about a woman who would be leaving in a few months—especially when he was dead set against love and marriage?

Aaron and Paul worked in silence for the rest of the morning, interrupted only by an English customer who dropped off two broken bridles and a worn-out harness that needed to be replaced. By noon, Aaron had James's saddle finished, and he'd also done some work at the riveting machine on a new harness.

"Think I'll head up to the house and see if your mamm's got lunch ready," Paul said as he headed for the door.

"You bringin' the food back, or should we close the shop and eat in Mama's kitchen today?" Aaron asked.

"I'll bring it back. Don't want to miss any customers that had planned to drop over during the noon hour." Paul nodded toward the finished saddle. "James Esh is one of them who'd said he'd be by." The door closed behind him, but a few minutes later, it opened again.

"Came by to get my saddle," James Esh announced as he stepped into the building. He wore a straw hat on his head, like all the Amish men in their area did during the summer. But James's hat was shaped a little different, and there was a bright red band tied around the middle.

"It's ready and waiting," Aaron said, motioning to the saddle lying on the workbench across the room.

James sauntered over to it and leaned close, like he was scrutinizing the work Aaron had done. "Hmm. Guess it's good enough."

Aaron bit back the unkind words that were on the tip of his tongue and moved over to Paul's desk. He reached into the metal basket and handed James his bill.

James squinted and clucked his tongue. "This is pretty high for just a cleanin' and oilin', wouldn't ya say?"

Aaron shrugged. "I don't set the prices. So if you've got a problem with the bill, you'd best take it up with Paul."

James glanced around the room. "Don't see him anywhere or I would."

"He went up to the house to get our lunch. You can wait if you've a mind to."

"Naw, I don't have any time to waste today." James reached into his pocket and pulled out a couple of large bills. He slapped the money down then sauntered back to his saddle, which he easily hoisted onto his broad shoulders.

He's just showin' off, Aaron fumed. *Always did like to act like he's tough as leather.*

James was almost to the door when he pivoted toward Aaron. "Say, did ya know that I escorted that new gal from Pennsylvania home from the singin' last night? Allison Troyer, that's her name."

Aaron gritted his teeth. Did James have to brag about everything he did? It seemed as if he was trying to rub salt in Aaron's wounds. But then, how could James know the way Aaron felt about him taking Allison home from the singing?

"That little woman sure is a cute one," James said with a crooked grin. "And her lips are soft as a kitten's nose."

Aaron's fingers made a fist as he fought for control. It would be wrong to provoke a fight, but he wanted more than anything to punch James in the nose. He took a deep breath and tried to relax. *He's only trying to get a rise out of me. I'd best let it go.*

"Yep, Allison's kiss was sweeter 'n honey." James wiggled his eyebrows and made a kissing sound as he puckered his lips.

Aaron took a step forward. "I don't believe you. Allison doesn't seem like the kind of woman who would let a man kiss her when they've only just met."

James's dark eyebrows lifted until they disappeared under his hat. "You callin' me a liar?"

Aaron was about to reply when the front door swung open and Paul stepped into the room, holding a wicker basket. "How are you, James?"

"Doin' real good," James replied with a nod.

"I see you've got what you came for." Paul motioned to the saddle perched on James's shoulders.

"Yep. I'm headed home with it now."

There was no mention of how much the cleaning and oiling had cost, and Aaron figured James had made an issue of it on his account. The ornery fellow had a knack for irritating folks. *Especially me. James has always known what it takes to get me riled up.*

"Well, I'd best be on my way. I might stop by the Kings' place and see if their niece wants to go on a picnic with me tomorrow afternoon." James had his back to Aaron now, so he couldn't see the fellow's face, but Aaron had a feeling there was a wily looking smile plastered there.

Paul placed the basket on the desk in front of Aaron. "You ready to eat, son?"

Aaron shook his head. "I ain't so hungry."

six

"Keep your legs pumping while you hold the material just so," Aunt Mary said as she showed Allison how to use her treadle sewing machine.

It looked easy when her aunt did it, but when Allison tried, things didn't go nearly so well. On her first attempt, she couldn't get the right momentum and kept pumping the treadle backward. Then, when she thought she had the hang of it, she went too fast and stitched right off the piece of cloth.

On Allison's next attempt, she stitched the end of her apron to the material. "I don't know how that happened," she muttered, repositioning the scrap of fabric.

"Try again," Aunt Mary encouraged. "You'll soon get the feel for it."

Allison lifted her feet and pumped up and down as she guided the wheel with one hand and directed the material with the other. When the thread snapped, so did her patience. "I'm no good at this!" She pushed her chair away from the machine and stood. "I'd rather do something else, if you don't mind."

Aunt Mary put her arm around Allison. "You'll catch on if you give it a chance. The more you practice, the better you'll get."

Allison shrugged. "Can it wait 'til later? It's such a nice day, and I'd like to go fishing if there's someplace nearby—and if I can borrow someone's pole."

"There's a pond up the road that has some good bass in it. I'm sure Harvey wouldn't mind if you used his pole. However, I don't think it's a good idea for you to go fishing alone."

"I'll be fine."

"Maybe so, but I'd feel better if you took one of your cousins along," her aunt insisted. "Dan's out in the garden pulling weeds with Sarah, but I'm sure he'd be happy to set his shovel aside and join you at the pond for a while."

Allison figured it wouldn't be so bad to have her ten-year-old cousin tag along. "Sounds gut to me," she said with a smile.

❧

Aaron rubbed a kink out of his lower back and glanced at the clock on the far wall. It was almost three thirty, and there hadn't been a single customer since noon. Paul had taken Mama, Grandpa, Grandma, and the girls into Springfield for the day. Joseph, Zachary, and Davey were helping one of the neighbors in their fields. That left Aaron alone in the shop, which was fine with him. However, he was tired of working, and for the last several days he'd been itching to do some fishing. Since things were slow, he decided there would be no harm in heading to the pond. The folks had said they might go out for supper after their shopping and appointments were done, so Aaron was sure they wouldn't be back until late evening. That left him plenty of time to get in a little fishing.

He removed his work apron, hung it on a wall peg, turned off the kerosene lanterns, and put the Closed sign in the front window. "Think I'll untie Rufus and take him along. The poor critter deserves some fun in the sun."

❧

Allison and Dan had been sitting on the grassy banks by the pond for nearly an hour without either of them getting a single bite. "Are you sure there's any fish in here?" Allison asked her young cousin.

Dan's head bobbed up and down. "Oh, jah. Me and Pa have taken many a good bass and plenty of catfish out of this pond."

She sighed. "Maybe they're just not hungry."

"We could move to a different spot," the boy suggested.

"You mean cast our lines in over there?" Allison pointed to the other side of the pond where a clump of bushes grew close together.

Dan shook his blond head, and his straw hat tipped to one side. "There's another pond about a mile down the road. Might be better fishin' there today."

Allison reeled in her line and stood. "I guess it's worth a try. You lead and I'll follow."

A short time later, they stood in front of the other pond. There were more trees growing nearby, which offered plenty of shade, and Allison decided that even if she didn't catch any fish, at least she would stay cool.

"Let's sit over there on one of them logs," Dan suggested.

Allison followed as he led her to the downed trees. She took a seat on one of the logs and had no more than thrown her line into the water when she heard a dog bark.

"Great! Now the fish will be scared away," Dan complained.

She glanced to her left and saw a young Amish man with a fishing pole step into the clearing. A collie romped beside him, barking and wagging its tail.

"Wouldn't ya know Aaron Zook would have to show up with that yappy dog of his?" Dan said with a scowl. "Now we'll never catch any fish."

Allison shielded her eyes from the glare of the sun. Sure enough, it was Aaron, and he seemed to be heading their way.

❧

Aaron's heart hammered when he realized it was Allison and her cousin Dan who sat on a log near the pond. He hadn't expected to run into anyone here—especially not her. With the exception of his mamm, most of the women he knew hated to fish. Maybe Allison had only come along to keep Dan company.

Rufus's tail swished back and forth, and he let out a couple of excited barks. Then the next thing Aaron knew, the dog took off on a run, heading straight for Allison.

"Come back here, Rufus!" Aaron shouted. The collie kept running, and by the time Aaron caught up to him, the crazy mutt had his head lying in Allison's lap.

She stroked the critter behind its ears and smiled up at Aaron.

"Sorry about that," he panted. "Don't know what got into that mutt of mine. I told him to stop, but he seems to take pleasure in ignorin' me."

"It's all right. I like friendly dogs."

Dan frowned and moved farther down the log. "Not me. Most dogs are loud and like to get underfoot." He pointed to his fishing pole. "And they scare away the fish with their stupid barking."

"Sorry," Aaron mumbled. "I'll try to make sure he stays quiet."

"Let Allison keep pettin' Rufus, and you won't have to worry about him barkin' or runnin' around."

Aaron hunkered down beside the log. "You could be right about that. I've never seen my dog take to anyone so quickly."

"I always wanted a dog," Allison murmured. "But Aunt Catherine wouldn't hear of it."

"You've got no dogs at your place?" Dan's raised brows showed his obvious surprise.

"Nope. Just a few cats to keep the mice down." Allison rubbed the end of Rufus's nose, and the dog burrowed his head deeper into her lap.

"Who's Aunt Catherine?" Aaron asked.

"She's my daed's older sister. She came to live with us soon after my mamm was killed."

Aaron's forehead wrinkled. "Mind if I ask how she died?"

"A car ran into her buggy." Allison frowned. "At least that's what I was told. I was only seven at the time and don't remember anything about the accident, even though I supposedly witnessed it."

"Sorry to hear that." Aaron started to bite his fingernail but stopped himself in time. "My real daed was killed the same way, and it was awfully hard on my mamm."

"I can't imagine losin' either one of my parents," Dan put in. "I'd miss 'em something awful."

Aaron nodded. "Jah. That's the way it goes."

❧

Tears stung the back of Allison's eyes, and she tried to think of something to talk about besides death. Truth was, the idea of dying scared her because she wasn't sure where her soul would go when it was time to leave this earth. Allison knew some folks felt confident that they'd go to heaven to be with Jesus, but she'd never understood how anyone could have that assurance. Did going to church every other Sunday guarantee that one would spend an eternity with the Lord, or could there be more to it?

"I—uh—guess if I'm going to fish, I'd better see about getting my hook baited," she said, pushing Rufus gently away.

The dog whined and flopped on the ground beside Allison, and she leaned over and picked up the jar of worms sitting next to Dan's feet. "Sure are fat little things, aren't they?" She held up the glass container and wrinkled her nose.

"Would you like me to put one on your hook?" Aaron asked, taking a seat on the log next to her.

"Thanks anyway, but I've been baiting my own hooks since I was a young girl." Allison's cheeks warmed, and she could have kicked herself for blurting that out. *Aaron must think I'm a real tomboy.*

Dan grunted and shot her a look of impatience. "If you two are gonna keep on yammerin', I'm movin' to the other side of the pond where it's quiet."

"No need to move; we'll quit talking." Allison baited her hook and cast the line into the water. Aaron did the same.

They sat in silence, with the breeze rustling the trees and Rufus's occasional snort being the only sounds.

"Did you enjoy the singing Sunday night, Allison?" Aaron asked suddenly.

"It was okay." She shifted on the log, almost bumping his arm. "Many of the songs were new to me, though."

"Not the same as you sing back home?"

"Just the hymns, but the others were different."

Dan grunted. "I thought we weren't gonna talk anymore."

Aaron scowled at the boy. "We sat here for quite a spell without sayin' a word, and nobody even had a nibble. So maybe a bit of chitchat might help to get the fish livened up."

"Puh!" Dan stood and moved to a large boulder several feet away.

"He thinks he knows a lot for someone so young," Aaron muttered. "Reminds me of the way James Esh used to be when he was a boy." He looked at Allison pointedly, but she made no comment.

"I noticed that you rode home with James after the singing."

She gave a quick nod and glanced at her cousin, who had lifted his face to the sun. *Sure hope Dan doesn't repeat any of this conversation when we get back to his house. I'd hate to explain things to Aunt Mary and Uncle Ben.*

"Somebody should have warned you about James," Aaron said.

"What do you mean?"

"He hasn't joined the church and is still in his rumspringa. To tell ya the truth, I wonder if he'll ever settle down and decide to be baptized."

"Some young people back home like to drink, smoke, and attend wild parties when they're going through rumspringa." Allison's forehead wrinkled. "And some leave the faith during that time and never come back."

"It's the same here," Aaron said. "But then many Amish who run wild during their teen years do settle down after a time." He released his grip on the pole and rubbed the bridge of his nose. "I think it's a sin and a shame the way some Amish kids hurt their families and get into all sorts of trouble during their running-around years."

"I take it you're not one of the rowdy ones?" she asked.

He shook his head. "I've never had the desire to do anything more than get involved in an occasional buggy race. For me, havin' fun means fishing, hunting, or playing ball."

"Same here," she blurted out. "I—I mean—"

"Hey, I've got a bite!" Dan hollered excitedly. He jumped off the rock and moved closer to the pond.

Allison cupped one hand around her mouth. "Be careful, Dan! You're gettin' awful near the water."

The boy looked over his shoulder, but his line jerked hard, and he lurched forward. *Splash*—into the water he went!

seven

On the drive home, Allison had a hard time keeping her thoughts from wandering. Until Dan had fallen into the pond, she'd been having fun—even without catching any fish. It had felt nice to sit in the warm sun and get to know Aaron a little better. He didn't brag on himself the way James had, and Allison thought if she had the opportunity to be with Aaron more, they might become friends. *Of course we could never be more than friends. Not unless I learn how to manage a home. Then maybe he might see me as someone he could possibly court.* She frowned. *With me only being here for the summer, I guess there wouldn't be much chance of us developing a lasting relationship, even if I were to become a woman someone might want to marry.*

"Are you mad at me?"

Dan's sudden question drove Allison's thoughts aside, and she turned to look at him. "Of course not. I know you didn't fall into the pond on purpose."

"That's for sure." Dan shivered beneath the quilt Allison had wrapped around his small frame. "That old catfish didn't wanna be caught, so he tried to take me into the water with him."

Allison laughed. "I think your foot slipped when the fish tugged on your line, and then you lost your balance."

Dan's forehead wrinkled. "Sure hope Mama won't be angry at me for gettin' my clothes all wet."

The boy's comment made Allison worry about her aunt's response. Would Aunt Mary be upset when she saw her waterlogged son? Would she blame Allison for the accident? Aunt Catherine certainly would have. She always thought everything was Allison's fault. Even something as silly as Aunt Catherine stubbing her toe on the porch step had been blamed on Allison; she'd been ahead of her aunt and was told she was walking too slowly.

Feeling the need to reassure the boy, Allison reached across the buggy seat and patted her cousin's knee. "I'll explain things to your mother."

"Danki."

Dan remained quiet for the rest of the ride, and Allison tried to keep her focus on driving the buggy and making sure the horse cooperated with her commands. The shoulder of the road wasn't as wide in this area as it was in most places she was familiar with back home. Of course there wasn't nearly as much traffic here, and for that she was glad.

When Allison guided the horse and buggy onto the Kings' property, she noticed a buggy parked out front and realized they must have company. *Good. If there's someone here visiting, Aunt Mary probably won't let on that she's mad when she finds out what happened to her boy.*

Dan climbed out of the buggy as soon as it came to a stop and hurried toward the house. Allison knew she should get the horse unhitched and into the barn right away, so she decided to let Dan tell his version of the pond mishap first.

❧

All the way home from the pond, Aaron thought about how much he had enjoyed being with Allison. Even if they couldn't develop a lasting relationship, it would be nice to enjoy her company while she was here for the summer. They'd had a good visit this afternoon, despite Dan's little mishap that had cut things short. Aaron was pleased to discover that Allison enjoyed many of the same things he did, too.

I wonder if Allison would enjoy working in the harness shop. Aaron slapped the side of his head, nearly knocking his straw hat off in the process. *Don't get any dumb ideas. It would never work, even if she could stay here. I wouldn't be able to forget what happened to my mamm when Papa died. I could never trust that it wouldn't happen to me.*

Aaron turned onto his property and noticed a light coming

from the harness shop. "Thought I shut off all the lanterns before I left."

He brought the horse to a stop in front of the building, hopped out of the buggy, and dashed inside. He discovered only one lantern lit—the one directly above Paul's desk.

Paul was seated in his oak chair, going over a stack of invoices spread before him. "Where have you been, Aaron?" he questioned.

Aaron shifted from one foot to the other, feeling like he was a young boy again. "I—uh—went fishing this afternoon."

Paul's heavy eyebrows drew together, and he fingered the edge of his full beard. "When you should have been working?"

"We hadn't had any customers since noon, so I didn't think there'd be any harm in closin' the shop a few hours."

Paul pushed his chair aside and stood. "I left you in charge today because I thought I could trust you to take care of things in my absence." He motioned to the front door. "Then I come home and find the shop door is locked, and the Closed sign is in the window."

Aaron opened his mouth to defend himself, but Paul cut him off. "I know you're expecting to take over this shop someday, but your irresponsible actions don't give me any indication that you'll be ready for quite some time."

"I work plenty hard, and I always do a good job," Aaron muttered.

Paul nodded. "That's true, but you're often late to work, and sometimes you look for excuses to slack off. You can't coast along in life if you expect to support a wife and a family someday."

"I don't think I am coastin'. Besides, I ain't ready for marriage yet." Aaron started to walk away but turned back around. "How come you're home early? I thought you were planning to eat supper out."

"Emma came down with a stomachache, so we came home earlier than planned."

Aaron felt concern for his youngest sister. "Has she got the flu?"

Paul shrugged. "I suppose she could, but more than likely she ate too much candy earlier in the day. Our driver, Gary Walker, always has a bag of chocolates he likes to hand out to the kinner, and Emma ate a whole handful before either your mamm or I realized it."

Aaron nodded. "I remember once when Davey was a little guy and got into Mama's candy dish. The *schtinker* polished off every last piece. Mama said she didn't have the heart to give him a *bletching* because his upset stomach was punishment enough."

Paul moved to the front of the desk and took a few steps toward Aaron. "Before you go up to the house, I'd like to say one more thing."

Out of respect, Aaron waited for his stepfather to continue, but he didn't like the feeling that Paul still saw him as a little boy rather than a twenty-year-old man.

"I love you, Aaron."

"Jah, I know."

"And that's the only reason I want to be sure you get your priorities straight."

Aaron felt his defenses rise again, but he knew it would be best to hold his tongue. "Is that all then?"

"Tell your mamm I'll be in for supper soon."

Aaron's only reply was a quick nod; then he opened the door and stepped quickly outside. "I ain't no baby," he muttered under his breath, "and I wish he'd quit treatin' me like one."

੨ઽ

Allison entered the house and was pleased to discover Katie Esh sitting at the kitchen table talking with Aunt Mary. "Sorry about bringing Dan home soaking wet," she apologized.

Aunt Mary smiled. "It's not the first time he's fallen into the pond, and it probably won't be the last. The little schtinker is upstairs now, taking a warm bath."

Allison looked down at the muddy footprints leading from the kitchen door to the hallway, and she clucked her tongue. "Since I'm the one who took Dan fishing, guess I'd better find the mop and clean the mess he left behind."

"Nonsense," her aunt said, pushing away from the table. "You sit with Katie and visit. I'll see to the floor."

Allison was amazed at her aunt's generosity. If this had happened in Aunt Catherine's kitchen, the woman would have been grumpier than an old goat.

Katie smiled and motioned to the chair beside her. "How about a glass of cold milk to go with the carrot cake I brought over?"

Allison glanced at Aunt Mary, who was already at the sink dampening the mop. "When are you planning to start supper?"

"Not for an hour or so. Ben, Harvey, and Walter will probably work in the fields until dark, so feel free to eat some of Katie's cake."

A hunk of moist carrot cake did sound appealing, so Allison poured a glass of milk from the pitcher in the center of the table and helped herself to a slice of the cake.

"I came by this afternoon to visit with you, but your aunt said you and Dan had gone fishing," Katie said.

"That's right, but sorry to say, we didn't catch a thing."

Katie giggled. "From the looks of Dan when he came through the door, I'd say the fish caught him instead."

Allison laughed, too. "Aaron and I rescued my waterlogged cousin before the fish could reel him in too far."

Katie's pale eyebrows lifted in obvious surprise. "Aaron Zook?"

"Jah."

"I didn't realize you were meeting him at the pond," Aunt Mary spoke up.

"Oh, I wasn't," Allison was quick to say. "He and his collie showed up, and it was shortly after they arrived that Dan fell in the water."

Katie gave Allison a knowing look, but she chose to ignore it. Instead, she forked a piece of cake into her mouth. "Umm. . . This is sure gut."

"I'm glad you like it."

"Next to chocolate, carrot's my favorite cake."

"What kind of pie do you like?" Katie asked.

"Most any, except for mincemeat."

Katie wrinkled her nose. "Me neither."

Aunt Mary swished the mop past the table and stopped long enough to grab a sliver of cake. "My favorite pie is strawberry."

Allison's mouth watered at the mention of sweet, juicy strawberries, so ripe they could melt in your mouth.

As if she could read Allison's mind, Katie leaned over and said, "We've got a big strawberry patch over at our place, and in a few more weeks they'll be ripe enough to pick. So, why don't you plan to come over some Saturday toward the end of the month?"

"That sounds like fun."

Katie reached over and patted Allison's hand. "In the meantime, let's set this Saturday afternoon aside, and the two of us can go on a picnic in the woods near my house. I'll furnish the whole meal."

Allison glanced at her aunt, who had finished her mopping and was now peeling potatoes at the kitchen sink. "Would that be all right with you, Aunt Mary?"

"I have no problem with it."

Allison smiled. She could hardly believe how agreeable her mother's twin sister seemed to be. She hated to compare Aunt Mary to Aunt Catherine, but they were as different as a contrary old hen and a sweet little lamb. What made the difference? What was the reason for Aunt Mary's loving, sweet disposition?

eight

Allison sat at the kitchen table, reading the letter she had just received from Papa. He seemed worried about her.

Dear Allison,
   I haven't heard from you except that one letter when you first arrived, and I was wondering why. I'm anxious to hear how things are going and what it's like there in Missouri.
   We're getting along okay here. We went to Gerald and Norma's for supper the other night, and all your brothers were there except Cleon and his family.

A wave of homesickness washed through Allison like a drenching rain. She'd always enjoyed spending time with her brothers, especially family dinners at one of their homes. All except Peter were married now, and he probably would be soon.
   I wonder if I'll ever marry, Allison mused. *Will I ever get over my tomboy ways enough for someone to fall in love with me?*
   Directing her focus back to the letter, she read on.

   Your aunt Catherine hasn't been feeling well. She's real tired and says there's a funny pain in her stomach. I suggested she see the doctor, but the stubborn woman flatly refuses. To tell you the truth, I think she misses you, and this is her way of showing it.

Allison shook her head. "No, Papa. Aunt Catherine doesn't miss me. If she did, she wouldn't have been so critical when I was there."
   "Were you speaking to me?" Aunt Mary asked as she stepped into the room.
   Allison's cheeks warmed. "I was reading a letter from my

daed that came in today's mail."

"How's my brother-in-law doing?" her aunt asked. "I'll bet he's missing you already."

"He says Aunt Catherine misses me, too, but I find that hard to believe."

Aunt Mary took a seat at the table. "Why would you say that, Allison?"

"Because Aunt Catherine has never shown much interest in me, except to find fault." Allison sniffed. "That's why I can't sew well."

Her aunt nodded. "Still, that's no reason to believe she doesn't care about you."

Allison's only reply was a slight shrug.

"Speaking of sewing," her aunt said, "would you like to try to make a faceless doll after we've had lunch?"

"You think I'm ready for that?"

"You've been practicing at the machine nearly every day this week, and you're able to sew a straight seam now. So I'd say you're ready to give it a try."

"Okay."

Aunt Mary patted Allison's hand. "I'll let you finish reading that letter while I go upstairs and finish my cleaning."

"Don't you need my help?"

"Sarah's helping, and you need time to reply to your daed's letter."

"I probably should, so Papa won't worry because he hasn't heard from me."

Aunt Mary clucked her tongue. "Guess it's my fault you've been too busy to write."

"No, it's not your fault. I've never been good about letter writing." Allison picked up her father's letter. "I'll do it as soon as I finish reading this."

❧

"Hey, Joseph. I thought you were out in the fields."

"I was," Aaron's brother replied as he stepped into the harness shop.

"What brings you here? Did ya break one of the mule's leather straps?"

"Came to see you, of course," Joseph said in a teasing voice.

Aaron chuckled and shook his head. "I'll bet you did."

Joseph grinned. "Actually it's Pop I came to see. Mama wanted me to tell him that she's hitchin' a horse to the buggy and will be takin' Emma into Seymour to see the doctor."

Aaron frowned. "Is our little sister still feelin' poorly?"

"Afraid so. As you know, she's been complaining of a bellyache for the last couple of days, and it don't seem to be goin' away."

"I thought it was just the flu."

"If it is, then it's lastin' much longer than most flu bugs." Joseph glanced around the room. "Where is Pop, anyway?"

Aaron motioned toward the back of the shop. "Paul's in the supply room, getting some things we'll be needin' to use later on."

"Okay, I'll give him Mama's message. Then I need to get back to the house and grab somethin' cold to drink for me, Zachary, and Davey." Joseph started to walk away, hesitated, and turned back around. "Say, I was wonderin' when and why you started callin' our daed by his first name."

"He ain't our real daed, Joseph. Have you forgotten that?"

"I know but we were just little when he married Mama, and we've been callin' him Pop ever since."

Aaron shrugged his shoulders. "In case you haven't noticed, I ain't little no more."

Joseph's eyebrows drew together, and the skin around his eyes crinkled. "No, but you sure don't act very grown-up at times." He took a step closer to Aaron. "What's Pop think of you callin' him Paul all of a sudden?"

"He hasn't said anything, so he probably doesn't care."

"I doubt that's the case, and I think you're silly." Joseph headed for the back room before Aaron could say anything more.

Aaron returned to his workbench and resumed work on the

bridle he was making for Gabe. "A lot you know, Joseph," he mumbled under his breath.

❧

"Is this the way the hair is supposed to attach to the doll's head?" Allison asked as she lifted the brown piece of material for her aunt's inspection.

Aunt Mary nodded. "You've got it pinned in exactly the right place."

Allison smiled. She knew *Hochmut*—pride—went against the Amish ways, but she couldn't help feeling rather pleased with herself.

"Now stitch that section of hair to the top of the head, and you'll be ready to put the rest of the body together."

Pumping her legs up and down and guiding the wheel of the treadle machine with one hand, Allison carefully sewed the hair in place.

"I'll be going to the farmer's market this Saturday to sell some of my quilted pillows," Aunt Mary said. "If you finish with the doll by then, maybe you'd like to come along. And if the doll sells, that might motivate you to make several more."

Allison finished the seam and cut the thread before she looked up. "I'd enjoy going to the farmer's market, but I'm supposed to go on a picnic with Katie this Saturday."

"Oh, that's right. I forgot."

"I'm looking forward to going to the farmer's market soon, though," Allison was quick to say. "Just not this Saturday, okay?"

"That's all right," her aunt said, giving Allison's shoulder a gentle squeeze. "Maybe by the time I go there again, you'll have more than one doll done."

"Jah, maybe so."

"Are you about ready to take a break? I thought a cold glass of Ben's homemade root beer would be good about now."

Allison smacked her lips. "That does sound refreshing." She stood and arched her back. "I think all that treadle pumping caused me to work up a thirst."

Aunt Mary chuckled. "Let's round up the kinner and have our snack out on the front porch. I'm sure they need a break from their garden chores."

A short time later, Allison, Aunt Mary, Sarah, and Dan sat in chairs on the front porch with tall glasses of root beer in their hands and a plate of peanut butter cookies filled to overflowing on the small table in front of them.

"This is sure gut." Dan made a slurping sound and swiped his tongue across his upper lip where some foamy root beer had gathered. "It would be even better if we had a batch of vanilla ice cream so's we could make ourselves a frosty float."

"That would be good. We'll have to see about making some homemade ice cream real soon," his mother said.

"How about this Saturday night?" Sarah suggested. "We can invite Grandpa and Grandma King over. What do you think about that, Mama?"

"That sounds like a fine idea, but you and I will be at the farmer's market all day Saturday. Maybe it would be best to wait until Sunday afternoon to make the ice cream."

"That's right," Dan put in. "It's an off-Sunday this comin' week, and there will be no preaching service."

Aunt Mary glanced at Allison and smiled. "Maybe we can have an outdoor barbecue and invite some of our friends and family. It would be a nice way of giving everyone the chance to get to know you better."

Allison's heart began to hammer. Would Aaron Zook and his family be included? She was tempted to ask but didn't want to let Aunt Mary or her cousins know she had an interest in Aaron. "A barbecue would be nice," she said.

"Can we invite the Hiltys?" Sarah asked. "I'd like my friend Bessie to be here."

"Jah, maybe so. And we can ask Gabe and Melinda Swartz." Aunt Mary smiled at Allison. "Melinda's about your age, but she wasn't at the last Sunday's preaching because she was sick that day." She eased out of her chair. "I'll pick up the ingredients we need for the ice cream while we're in Seymour on Saturday. But for now, I think I'd better see about making some corn bread and beans for our supper."

Allison started to get up, but her aunt motioned her to sit back down. "Take your time and finish your root beer. When you're done, you can make the coleslaw while Sarah sets the table."

Allison had never made coleslaw before, but she'd seen Aunt Catherine do it and figured it couldn't be that hard. Just chop up some cabbage, add a little mayonnaise, some vinegar, salt, and pepper. Seemed easy enough to her.

nine

Allison watched with anticipation as Uncle Ben forked some of her coleslaw into his mouth. After the first bite, he puckered his lips and quickly reached for his glass of water. "Whew! Why is there so much vinegar in this?" He looked over at his wife, like he thought she was the one responsible for it.

"I don't think there's that much," Aunt Mary said with a shrug. She spooned some onto her plate and took a bite. Her eyes widened, although she never said a negative word, just swallowed it down.

"Papa's right. This stuff is awful!" Dan jumped up from the table and ran over to the garbage can, where he spit out the coleslaw he had put in his mouth.

Allison's face burned with embarrassment. She couldn't even make a simple thing like coleslaw without ruining it. "I–I'm sorry," she stammered. "Guess I should have asked how much vinegar to use."

"You mean *you* made the coleslaw?" Walter asked, pointing at Allison.

She nodded as tears sprang to her eyes. "I thought it would be easy, but I guess I was wrong."

"What were you tryin' to do, make us all sick?" Walter wrapped his fingers around his throat and coughed as though he were gagging.

"There's too much pepper in it, too." Sarah sputtered and gulped half of her water down.

"That will be enough about the coleslaw," Uncle Ben said sternly. "I'm sure Allison didn't ruin it on purpose. The vinegar probably spilled from the bottle before she realized what had happened."

"Yeah," Harvey put in. "I tried pouring some of that stuff

58

onto a piece of cotton when I got a nosebleed a couple weeks ago, and it ran out all over the counter."

Allison knew her aunt, uncle, and oldest cousin were trying to make her feel better, but their comments hadn't helped at all. "No wonder Aunt Catherine never let me do much in the kitchen," she mumbled. "She was afraid I'd make everyone sick."

"I'm sure that's not true," Aunt Mary said kindly. "All you need is a little more practice. Why, by the end of the summer you'll be cooking so well that your Aunt Catherine will be happy to let you take over her kitchen."

"I doubt she'd let anyone take her place in the kitchen." Allison sniffed. "Besides, it's not just cooking I can't do well. There are many other things I haven't learned about running a house."

"With my wife as your teacher," Uncle Ben said, looking over at Aunt Mary and giving her a wink, "I can almost guarantee that you'll be ready to get married and run a house of your own by the end of summer."

Sarah giggled. "Now we just need to find her a husband."

❧

The telephone on Paul's desk rang sharply, and Aaron reached for it, since Paul was outside talking to a customer. "Zook's Harness Shop," he said into the receiver. At least Paul hadn't insisted on changing the name of their business to Hilty after he'd married Aaron's mamm. And he'd been the one to suggest they put a phone in the shop, since it wasn't allowed inside their Amish home.

"Aaron, is that you?" He recognized his mother's voice and knew she was upset about something.

"Jah, Mom, it's me. What's wrong?"

"Would you please put Paul on the phone?"

"He's outside talkin' to Noah Hertzler right now. Can I give him a message?"

"The doctor thinks Emma's problem is her appendix. He wants us to take her to the hospital right away."

Aaron gripped the receiver tightly. "If it bursts open, she

could be in big trouble, isn't that right?"

"I'm afraid so."

"So are you wantin' Paul to hire a driver and pick you and Emma up in Seymour, or are you comin' home first?"

"There's no time to waste. I've hired a driver in town, so please ask your daed to get a driver and meet us at the hospital in Springfield."

"Okay, Mom. And I'll be praying for Emma."

"Danki."

Aaron hung up the phone and dashed outside to give Paul the news. "Mom just called, and she wants you to hire a driver and meet her and Emma at the hospital in Springfield."

"What?" Paul's forehead wrinkled. "Why are they going to the hospital?"

"The doctor thinks Emma's appendix is about to burst, so Mom hired a driver to take them to the hospital."

Paul's face blanched, and he turned to Noah. "Sorry, but I've gotta go."

"Of course you do. We can talk some other time." Noah headed for his buggy, calling over his shoulder, "We'll be praying for Emma, and be sure to let us know how she's doing."

"We will." Paul nodded at Aaron. "Run back inside and phone one of our English neighbors about givin' me a ride to Springfield. I'll go up to the house and let your mamm's folks know what's happening. Bessie can help Grandma get supper going while your brothers finish helping the neighbor in his fields."

"What do you need me to do after I'm done making the phone call?" Aaron asked.

"Complete whatever you're working on in the harness shop." Paul gave his beard a couple of pulls. "Then maybe you should hang out here the rest of the evening so you can answer the phone. We'll be wantin' to let you know how things are going at the hospital."

"Jah, okay. By the time you get back from the house I'll have a driver lined up for you."

His stepfather gave a quick nod then sprinted toward the house.

Aaron sent up a quick prayer and rushed back to the harness shop.

❧

Aaron paced in front of Paul's desk, waiting for some word on his sister's condition. Paul had phoned shortly after he'd gotten to the hospital, saying the doctors had determined it was Emma's appendix and she'd be going in for surgery soon. That was several hours ago, and Aaron was getting worried.

At six o'clock, Joseph had brought out a meat loaf sandwich, but that still sat on the desk, untouched. Aaron had no appetite for food. Not when his little sister's life could be in jeopardy. He'd tried to get some work done, but all he could do was pray and pace.

At nine o'clock, the phone rang, and he grabbed for the receiver. "Zook's Harness Shop." He didn't know why he was answering it that way. Nobody would be calling the shop at this time of night for anything related to business.

"Hi, Aaron, it's Mom. I wanted to let you know that Emma's out of surgery now, but she's still in the recovery room."

"How'd it go?"

"The doctor said things are looking good, and she should recover fine."

"Had her appendix burst?"

"No, but it was getting close."

Aaron released a puff of air. "I'm glad you got her there in time."

"So are we." There was a brief pause, and Aaron could hear his mother say something to Paul, but he couldn't make out the words. A few seconds later, she said into the phone, "We've decided to stay here all night. Could you make sure Grandma and Grandpa are okay and settled in at the *daadihaus*?"

"Sure, Mom. I'll head up to their house right now and check

on them."

"Paul said to tell you to open the shop without him in the morning, because we're not sure how long we'll be here."

"No problem. I can manage fine on my own."

"Danki, Aaron. I knew we could count on you."

"I'll be here bright and early tomorrow, so let me know if you need anything," he said. "I could hire a driver and send one of the brothers or close the shop and come to the hospital myself."

"We'll let you know, son."

"Okay. Bye, Mom."

"Good night."

Aaron hung up the phone and sank onto the wooden stool behind the desk. He let his head fall forward in his hands. "Thank You, Lord, for bringing Emma through her surgery. Now please help her to heal quickly."

ten

"I hope Bessie and her whole family can come to our barbecue on Sunday," Sarah said to Allison as they sat beside each other in one of her daed's open buggies. They were heading toward the Hiltys' place, and Allison was driving the horse.

Allison only nodded in response to her cousin's comment. She didn't want the girl to know how much she hoped Aaron would come.

"Sure will be fun to have some homemade ice cream," Sarah said, smacking her lips.

"Does your family make it often?" Allison asked.

"Jah, lots of times during the summer. Doesn't your family make ice cream?"

"We do on occasion, but since most of my brothers are married now, we don't make it as much as we did when they all lived at home."

"The only part of ice cream makin' I don't like is the crankin'," Sarah said, wrinkling her nose.

Allison grinned. "That can be hard, especially toward the end when the ice cream starts to freeze up."

They rode in companionable silence the rest of the way and soon pulled into the Hiltys' place. They discovered Bessie sitting under a tree in the front yard, and as soon as Allison brought the buggy to a stop, Sarah jumped out and ran over to her friend.

Allison tied the horse to the hitching post near the barn and joined the girls on the lawn. She'd been tempted to drop by the harness shop to see Aaron but couldn't think of a good excuse to go there.

"I invited Bessie to our barbecue on Sunday, but she's not sure if they can come," Sarah said with a shake of her head.

Allison felt disappointment all the way to her toes. "I'm sorry to hear that."

"It's not that we don't wanna come, but my little sister's in the hospital," Bessie explained. "Her appendix got sick, and she had to have it taken out."

"Will she be okay?" Allison remembered the day her brother Peter's appendix had ruptured. He'd been thirteen at the time, and Papa was afraid he might not make it. But after several days in the hospital, Peter had recovered nicely.

"I think so. Emma's gonna be in the hospital awhile, and the folks will be goin' back and forth to see her." Bessie turned to Sarah. "That means they probably won't be able to go over to your place on Sunday."

"Say, I've got an idea," Sarah said to her friend. "Maybe one of your brothers could bring you to the barbecue."

Bessie grabbed Sarah's hand. "Aaron's in the harness shop. Let's go see if he thinks all the brothers might go."

The girls trotted off, and Allison willingly followed. She was pleased for the chance to say hello to Aaron.

❧

Struggling with an oversized piece of leather, Aaron looked up when the front door swooshed opened. He was surprised to see Bessie step inside the harness shop with Sarah and Allison.

"Hey, Aaron. Look who's here," his sister said.

"What brings you by the harness shop on this hot Friday morning?" Aaron asked, looking at Allison.

"They came to invite us to a barbecue at their place on Sunday afternoon," Bessie replied before Allison could open her mouth.

Aaron dropped the hunk of leather to his workbench and stepped forward. "Didn't you tell them about Emma?"

"Of course I did."

"Then you know our little sister will probably still be in the hospital come Sunday, and I'm sure the folks won't be goin' anywhere except to Springfield to see her."

"I realize that," Bessie said in an exasperated tone. "But that don't mean we can't go to the barbecue."

Aaron glanced at Allison again, and she offered him a pleasant smile. "Your sister thought maybe you and your brothers could bring her over," she said.

"That's a nice idea," Aaron replied, "but somebody's gotta stay here with Grandma and Grandpa Raber."

Bessie's lower lip protruded. "I'm sure they can manage on their own for a couple of hours."

Aaron shifted from one foot to the other as he contemplated the idea. Grandpa's arthritis had gotten so bad over the years he could barely walk, and Grandma's bad back made it difficult for her to do much. While it was true that they could survive a few hours alone, he would feel better if someone were at home in case a need arose.

"I'll talk to Mom about it when she and Paul get back from the hospital later today. If they don't mind you going, at least one of us brothers can drive you over to the Kings' on Sunday."

"Danki." Bessie hugged Aaron, then reached for Sarah's hand. "While you're here, would you like to go out to the barn and see the new baby goat that was born a few days ago?"

"Sure!" Sarah turned to Allison. "Would ya like to come along?"

Allison hesitated but then shook her head. "You two go along. I think I'll stay and visit with Aaron awhile."

Sarah and Bessie scampered out the door, and Allison moved toward the workbench where Aaron stood. He was pleased that she'd chosen to stick around.

"Are you minding the shop on your own today?" she questioned.

"Jah. Probably will be 'til Emma's out of the hospital."

She leaned closer. "Is harness making hard work?"

"Sometimes, but I enjoy what I do." Aaron motioned to the piece of leather lying before him. "It's a gut feeling to take a hunk of this stuff and turn it into something useful like a bridle or a harness."

"The harness shop back home repairs shoes, too," Allison said.

"Is that the one Paul's cousin owns?"

"I believe it is."

"Paul thought about doin' that here, but we get enough business with just saddles, harnesses, and bridles, so I doubt he'll ever do shoes."

Allison drew in a deep breath as she scanned the room. "I can't get over how nice it smells in here."

He smiled. "You really think so?"

"I do. In fact, I think it would be fun to work in a place like this."

"You might not say that if you knew what all was involved."

She leaned on the workbench and studied the piece of leather. "Why don't you show me?"

He skirted around beside her. "All right, I will."

With a feeling of excitement, Aaron showed Allison around the shop, demonstrating how he connected a breast strap to a huge three-way snap that required some fancy looping, pointing out numerous tools they used in the shop, and showing her two oversized sewing machines run by an air compressor.

"Wow, these are much bigger than the treadle machine Aunt Mary uses." Allison smiled. "She's been teaching me how to sew, and I've learned to make a faceless doll."

"I'll bet that required some hand stitching, too."

She nodded. "Tiny snaps had to be sewn on the clothes."

"Nothin' like the big ones we use here." He nodded toward the riveting machine. "That's how we punch shiny rivets into our leather straps."

Allison followed as he moved to the front of the store. "What were you working on when we first came in?"

"I was getting ready to cut some leather, but the thing's so long and heavy, I may need to wait 'til Paul's here and can help me with it."

Allison's eyes lit up like a couple of copper pennies. "I'd be happy to help."

"You wouldn't mind holding one end while I do the cutting?"

"Not at all. I think it would be fun."

Aaron could hardly believe it. Here was a woman just like his mamm, who seemed eager and willing to help in the harness shop.

Allison held one end of the leather piece while Aaron made the necessary cuts. They had just finished when Sarah and Bessie returned to the shop.

"Are you ready to go?" Sarah asked Allison. "We told Mama we'd only be gone a little while."

Allison seemed reluctant to let go of the leather. "I suppose we should be on our way."

Aaron followed them to the door. "Thanks for your help. Maybe I'll see you on Sunday."

Bessie stared up at him with a questioning look. "Are you thinkin' you might be the one who takes me to the Kings' barbecue?"

He shrugged. "Maybe so."

Allison grinned and headed out the door. Aaron returned to his work, whistling a happy tune.

eleven

"I'm glad you were free to go on a picnic with me this evening," Katie said to Allison as they rode in Katie's open buggy toward one of the ponds off Highway C. "This will give us a chance to get to know each other better."

"Sorry we couldn't have left earlier, but Aunt Mary needed my help cleaning the house and getting things ready for tomorrow's barbecue before she and Sarah left for the farmer's market."

"That's okay. I had plenty of chores to do at my place today, too." Katie flicked the reins, and the horse broke into a trot. "I'm glad I got an invitation to your aunt and uncle's barbecue." She smiled. "You mentioned that the Hiltys were invited, so I'm hoping Joseph Zook will be there, too."

And I hope his brother Aaron will come, Allison secretly thought. "You've heard about little Emma being in the hospital, haven't you?"

"Jah, it's a shame about her appendix."

"Sarah and I stopped by the harness shop yesterday to invite the family to the barbecue. That's when Aaron said he wasn't sure if any of them could come. He did say he or one of his brothers might bring Bessie over, though."

"If only one brother can come, I hope it will be Joseph."

Allison chuckled. One thing she'd learned about Katie was that she had a one-track mind, and it led to one place—Joseph Zook.

"Sure is a pretty evening," Katie commented as they pulled into a grassy area near the pond. "It's much cooler now than it was earlier in the day."

"It's been hot and muggy all week," Allison said. "But I should be used to it, because we have the same kind of weather in Lancaster County during the summer months."

Katie halted the horse. "Would you mind getting the picnic basket from the backseat while I tether Sandy to a tree?"

"Sure, I can do that." Allison climbed down from the buggy and reached under the seat. She grasped the wicker basket with one hand and the quilt lying beside it with the other hand. As soon as Katie had the horse secured, they headed for the pond.

A few minutes later, they were seated on the quilt eating their picnic supper, which consisted of crispy fried chicken, deviled eggs sprinkled with paprika, tangy dill pickles, and fresh, cool potato salad. Katie had also brought a thermos of iced tea, and for dessert, a pan full of brownies with thick chocolate frosting.

"Everything tastes so gut," Allison said, blotting her lips on a napkin. "I wish I could cook as well as you do."

Katie tipped her head and stared at Allison as though perplexed. "I thought all Amish women could cook well. Most Amish girls learn to cook at a young age, isn't that so?"

"Not me. Aunt Catherine has never allowed me to do much in the kitchen."

"Really?"

Allison nodded. "My aunt likes to be in charge of things. She often says she can't be bothered with the messes I make in her kitchen."

"How does she expect you to learn the necessary things in order to run a house of your own someday?"

"I don't know, but Aunt Mary apparently doesn't think that way. She's more than willing to teach me how to cook and sew." Allison wrinkled her nose. "I don't know if I'll ever learn, though. You should have tasted the awful coleslaw I made the other night. I put too much vinegar in, and I'm sure everyone at the table thought I was trying to make them sick."

Katie snickered. "I doubt anyone thought that."

Allison reached for another drumstick and was about to take a bite when she heard voices nearby. That's when she noticed another buggy parked next to Katie's and saw two young Amish men with fishing poles heading toward the pond. Her heart skipped a beat. It was Aaron and his brother, Joseph.

Katie jumped up and ran over to them. "Allison and I are having a picnic supper. Would you like to join us?"

Allison waved at Aaron, and he lifted his hand in response. "We've already had our supper," he told Katie. "Joseph and I want to do a little fishing, so don't let us bother you."

"It won't be a bother," she insisted.

"See, Aaron, they don't mind us joining them. Besides, I could eat a little something," Joseph was quick to say.

Aaron thumped his younger brother on the back. "You must have a hollow leg."

Joseph merely shrugged, leaned his fishing pole against a nearby tree, and followed Katie back to the quilt.

Allison anxiously waited to see what Aaron would do and was pleased when he followed them.

"Did you bring your fishing pole along?" Aaron asked Allison as he took a seat on the edge of the quilt closest to her. Of course Aaron had no place else to sit, since Joseph had plunked down right next to Katie.

"I didn't bring a pole. Katie and I just came to eat and enjoy our time together," Allison replied. The truth was, she was glad Aaron hadn't caught her fishing again. She was embarrassed enough that he'd seen how much she enjoyed helping him in the harness shop yesterday. *I'll never get a man if I keep acting like a tomboy,* she chided herself.

"And then we showed up and ruined your picnic," Joseph said with a snicker. He winked at Katie, and she swatted him playfully on the arm.

It was obvious that the two of them cared for each other, and Allison felt a stab of jealousy. She had no steady boyfriend back home, and even if she found one here, she wouldn't be staying long enough to establish a lasting relationship.

"How's your little sister doing?" Allison asked Aaron. "Is she still in the hospital?"

He nodded. "She's gettin' along well but probably won't come home until early next week."

"I'm glad she's going to be okay."

"Me, too."

"Will either of you be going to the barbecue at Allison's aunt and uncle's tomorrow afternoon?" Katie asked, changing the subject. She looked at Joseph and then over at Aaron.

"I thought I might go," they said at the same time.

Everyone laughed.

"I guess Zachary and Davey are planning to stay home with Grandma and Grandpa since Mom and Paul will probably be at the hospital visiting Emma during that time," Aaron said.

"Yeah, that's right," Joseph agreed. "You and me get to escort Bessie to the barbecue." He grinned at Katie. "Will you be there?"

She nodded. "Definitely."

The foursome continued to visit while Allison and Katie finished eating their supper. Joseph helped himself to some chicken and potato salad, but Aaron said he was still full from supper.

When they were done eating and everything had been put away, the men invited the women to join them at the pond.

Aaron squatted beside Allison and extended his pole. "Would you like to fish awhile?"

She smiled and eagerly reached for it but pulled her hand back in time. "I—I'd better just watch."

"How come?"

"Uh—fishing isn't very ladylike."

"My mamm likes to fish, and she's a real lady. Of course she doesn't go as often as she used to now that my grandma and grandpa need her more."

"Don't you have other family to help with their care?" she asked.

"My brothers and I try to help out as much as we can, just like we've been doing this week while Emma's in the hospital." Aaron wedged his pole between his knees, leaned back on his elbows, and lifted his face toward the sky. "Ever wonder what heaven is like?"

"Sometimes." The truth was, Allison thought about heaven a lot, wondering whether she would ever get there. Even though she had attended church since she was a baby, she'd never felt as if she knew God in a personal way. For that matter, Allison didn't think He knew her, either. She envied people like Aunt Mary, who prayed out loud and seemed to walk closely with the Lord on a daily basis. She often wondered how her mother had felt about spiritual things when she was alive. *Maybe I should have asked Papa about that.*

"I hope there will be fishin' holes like this in heaven," Aaron said.

Allison was about to reply when Aaron leaned forward and hollered, "Hey! I've got a bite!"

She watched with envy as he gripped his pole and started playing the fish. "I think it's a big one!" he hollered.

"Don't fall in the water like my cousin Dan did awhile back."

"I won't; don't worry." Aaron moved closer to the edge of the pond, reeling in his catch a little at a time. Soon a nice-sized bass lay at his feet, and he knelt beside it with a satisfied smile.

Can I remove the hook? Allison almost offered. But she caught herself before the words popped out. She glanced over at Katie, who sat beside Joseph with a contented smile. Katie didn't seem the least bit interested in fishing, but she could cook, and if that's what a man wanted in a wife, then Allison would learn to do the same.

Aaron extended the pole toward Allison. "Now it's your turn."

"What?"

"I thought maybe you'd changed your mind and would like to catch a few fish."

Allison drew in a deep breath, savoring the musty aroma of the pond and the fishy smell of the bass he'd landed. Oh, how she longed to grip that fishing pole and throw the line into the water. It would feel so satisfying to snag a big old bass or tasty catfish. "I'll just watch," she mumbled.

"Okay." Aaron cast out his line once more, and they sat in silence for a while.

Allison could hardly contain herself when Aaron reeled in another bass, followed by a couple of plump catfish.

"Hey, Joseph," he called to his younger brother, "I'll bet you can't top the size of my last fish!"

"I'm not tryin' to," Joseph shot back. "I've got three nice catfish, and I ain't one bit worried about their size."

Aaron chuckled. "All my brother worries about is tryin' to make an impression on Katie Esh." His face sobered. "Speaking of the Esh family. . . Katie's cousin James isn't comin' to your barbecue tomorrow, is he?"

"I don't know who all my aunt and uncle have invited."

"It would be just my luck if James was there." Aaron bit off the end of a fingernail and spit it onto the ground.

Allison wrinkled her nose. "Do you have to do that? I think it's *ekelhaft*."

Aaron examined his hands and frowned. "You're right. It is a disgusting habit, and I do it whenever I'm nervous or upset about something."

"Would you be upset if James came to the barbecue?"

"Guess I would, but it's not my decision who comes or not."

Allison wasn't sure what Aaron had against James, but she, too, hoped the arrogant fellow would not be at the barbecue.

twelve

Allison didn't know why, but thinking about the barbecue that would begin in less than an hour made her feel jittery as a June bug. Maybe it was because she was excited about seeing Aaron again. Or the butterflies doing a dance in her stomach could be from worry over who else might be in attendance.

"If James shows up, I'll just ignore him," she muttered as she sliced a batch of tomatoes Aunt Mary had set on the cupboard a few minutes ago.

"What was that?"

Allison whirled around. She'd thought she was alone in the kitchen. Aunt Mary had gone outside to see if Uncle Ben had the barbecue lit. Sarah and Dan were supposed to be setting the picnic tables. Walter was outside somewhere. And she'd certainly never expected Harvey to come into the kitchen. But here he was, looking at her like she'd taken leave of her senses.

"I—uh—was talkin' to myself," she mumbled, quickly turning back to the counter where she continued to cut the tomatoes into thin slices.

He chuckled. "No need to look so flustered. We all talk to ourselves sometimes."

Allison smiled. She still couldn't get over how easygoing this family seemed to be. If Aunt Catherine had caught Allison talking to herself, she would have made an issue. In this home, everyone seemed relaxed and accepting of one another.

"I came in to get the hamburger rolls," Harvey said, moving toward the ample-sized bread box where Aunt Mary kept all of her baked goods.

"Have any of the guests arrived yet?" Allison asked.

He shook his head. "Not that I know of, but I'm sure they'll be here soon."

"And you don't know who all is coming?"

"Nope. Just heard that Mom and Dad had invited the Hiltys, Eshes, Swartzes, and Hertzlers."

"Which Eshes?"

Harvey shrugged. "Not sure."

Allison went to the refrigerator and removed a jar of pickles. "I guess we'll know soon enough."

"Yep." Harvey started across the room. "Mom said to tell ya to bring out the stuff you're cuttin' up as soon as you're done."

"I will." Allison turned back to her chore as Harvey went out the back door. *Now if I can just get myself calmed down enough to relax and have a good time. It's just plain silly to get all worked up over who's coming and who's not.*

❧

Aaron clucked to his buggy horse to get him moving faster then glanced over at Joseph, who sat on the seat beside him. Bessie was in the back and had been practicing her yodeling ever since they'd left home. Earlier today his sister had told him that Melinda Swartz, Gabe's wife, was teaching her some special yodeling techniques.

Aaron was glad Davey and Zachary had been willing to stay home with Grandma and Grandpa today. That left him and Joseph free to escort Bessie to the Kings' barbecue. It also meant he would see Allison again, and that thought pleased him more than he cared to admit. He'd never met anyone like her before, and if he weren't so set against marriage, he might want to court her. Then again, since she would be returning to Pennsylvania at the end of summer, what harm could there be in them doing a few things together? Since Allison wouldn't be staying in Webster County, she'd have no expectations of love or romance. *Maybe I should ask her out. If I can get up the nerve, and we have some time alone, I might do it today at the barbecue.*

"You're awfully quiet," Joseph said, breaking into Aaron's thoughts.

"It's kind of hard to talk with Bessie in the backseat, cacklin' away."

Joseph chuckled. "You're right about that." He glanced over his shoulder. "Our little sister seems determined to master the art of yodeling."

"She'll need a lot more practice if she's to accomplish that," Aaron said with a grunt.

"Melinda started yodeling when she was a girl, and she does it well. I'm sure in time Bessie will get the hang of it."

"You could be right."

"I don't know about you, but I'm sure lookin' forward to the barbecue and all that gut food." Joseph gave his stomach a couple of pats.

"More than likely what you're really lookin' forward to is spending time with Katie Esh."

"That, too."

"You thinkin' of marryin' the girl?"

Joseph's ears turned pink. "Maybe someday, but not 'til we're both a little older, and certainly not 'til I can find myself a better job."

"You're not happy workin' at the Christmas tree farm or doin' part-time field work for the neighbors?"

"Not really. Don't think I'd want to spend the rest of my life flaggin' trees, pullin' thorny weeds, or traipsin' through the dusty fields behind a pair of stubborn mules."

"Noah Hertzler has worked at Osborn's Christmas Tree Farm for several years, and he seems happy enough."

"Jah, well, one man's pleasure is another man's pain."

"You hate it that much?"

"I don't hate it. Just don't like it well enough to keep doin' it forever." Joseph looked over at Aaron. "I need somethin' that provides more of a challenge—the way your work in the harness shop does."

Aaron frowned. "You're wanting to work in the harness shop now? You've never shown any interest in it before."

Joseph laid a hand on Aaron's arm. "I'm not after your job. I'd just like to find somethin' that's more of a challenge for me."

Aaron drew in a breath and released it quickly. It was a relief to know his brother didn't want to work at the harness shop. If he did, Paul might decide to turn the shop over to Joseph someday and not Aaron. Of course, there was always Zachary and Davey to consider. One of them might want in on their real daed's shop.

"Maybe you should consider carpentry or painting as a trade," Aaron suggested. "There's always a need for that."

"Might like to work on a dairy or chicken farm."

Aaron knew Allison's daed ran a dairy farm with one of his sons, but he didn't figure Joseph would want to move to Pennsylvania and leave Katie behind, so he decided not to mention the idea. In all likelihood, his younger brother would probably try several other jobs before he found the one that worked best for him.

"Oddle-lei-de-tee! Oddle-lei-de-tee!" Bessie's shrill voice grew louder and louder, until Aaron thought he would scream.

"Would ya quiet down back there? I can hardly think, and your howlin' is giving me a headache."

Bessie quieted immediately, but Aaron figured it was because she was afraid he might turn around and head back home. Of course he wouldn't, because he was anxious to see Allison, but he wasn't about to tell his little sister that.

A short time later, they pulled onto the Kings' property, and Aaron parked the buggy near the barn. He put his horse in the corral while Joseph walked Bessie up to the house. "I'll be there soon," he called.

"Jah, okay," Joseph said with a wave.

౨ఎ

Allison stepped onto the back porch in time to see Bessie Hilty and her brother Joseph walk into the yard. Disappointment flooded her soul when she realized Aaron wasn't with them. She'd hoped he would come to the barbecue but figured he must have responsibilities that kept him at home.

At least Katie will be happy when she arrives and sees that Joseph is here, Allison thought. *Guess I shouldn't be so* missvergunnisch— *envious—but it's hard to see Katie and Joseph all smiles when they're together.*

Determined to be pleasant, Allison stepped forward and greeted her guests. "Sarah's in the house helping Aunt Mary with the lemonade. She'll be glad to see you."

"I'll go inside and help them." Bessie bounded away and Allison turned to Joseph. "You and Bessie are the first to arrive, but I'm sure Katie and her family will be here shortly."

Joseph grinned. "Glad to hear it."

Allison motioned to the barbecue across the lawn. "Uncle Ben's got the chicken cooking, and he'll be doing up some burgers, too. We should be able to eat soon."

"It sure smells gut." Joseph sniffed the air. "Guess I'll wander over there and say hello."

He sauntered off, and Allison moved over to the picnic tables. She'd only taken a few steps when she spotted Aaron coming out of the barn. Her heart did a little flip-flop, and she drew in a quick breath to steady her nerves.

"When Bessie and Joseph showed up without you, I didn't think you'd come," she told Aaron when he walked into the backyard.

"I put my horse in the corral then stopped off at the barn to talk to Harvey and Walter. They were checking on the new horse their daed recently bought."

Allison smiled. "I'm glad you could be here."

"Me, too." Aaron glanced around, like he might be feeling nervous. "Where is everyone? Are we the only ones here?"

"You, Joseph, and Bessie are the first guests to arrive, but the others should be along soon, I expect."

Aaron shifted from one foot to the other and stared at the ground.

"Would you like to sit down?"

"Sure, I—I guess so."

Aaron took a seat on one of the picnic benches, and Allison sat across from him. Feeling suddenly nervous herself, Allison fiddled with the napkin in front of her. *I wonder if Aaron only came because he felt obligated to bring Bessie. But if that's true, why didn't he just let Joseph bring their sister?*

Aaron cleared his throat, and Allison jumped. "Uh, I was wondering. . ."

"Yes?"

"Do you think you might be free to—?"

Aaron's words were halted when a buggy rolled into the yard and a deep male voice hollered, "Whoa there! Hold up, you crazy critter!"

Allison's mouth dropped open when she saw James Esh in his fancy buggy, with his unruly horse trotting at full speed straight for the barn.

thirteen

Allison sat at the picnic table between Katie and James. She felt miserable and couldn't believe how terribly things had gone so far. First, James had arrived in a cloud of dust and nearly ran his horse into the side of her uncle's barn. Fortunately, he'd pulled back on the reins soon enough, but it had been a close call. Then, when Allison and Aaron dashed across the yard to see if James and the horse were all right, James made a couple of rude remarks and said he was only trying to give them a thrill. It had been a thrill, all right. One Allison could have easily done without.

After that, the other guests arrived, and everyone was called over to the picnic tables. Allison wasn't happy when James plunked down beside her, but she didn't let on.

I'd much rather be sitting next to Aaron. She glanced at the other table to the left of them. Aaron sat beside his sister, and she noticed that he'd barely touched anything on his plate.

Gabe and Melinda Swartz sat across from Aaron, looking happy and content. Katie and Joseph were all smiles, too, and Allison couldn't help envying the two couples who were obviously in love.

Will any man ever look at me the way Joseph looks at Katie? Will I ever fall in love? And if I do, will I learn enough about running a house so I can be married?

"Maybe you young people would like to play a game of croquet after we're done eating," Aunt Mary suggested, smiling at Allison. "Later, after everyone feels hungry again, we'll get started on the homemade ice cream."

"Croquet sounds like fun," Katie spoke up. She turned to Joseph. "Don't you think so?"

He nodded with an eager expression. "I've always enjoyed battin' the ball around."

Allison snickered, and Katie jabbed Joseph in the ribs. "It's not baseball we'll be playing, silly. We're supposed to hit the ball through the metal wickets, using a mallet."

Joseph wiggled his eyebrows. "I knew that."

Allison felt James's warm breath on her neck as he leaned over and whispered, "Why don't you and me take a walk down the road while the others play their silly game? We can get to know each other better if we're alone."

The back of Allison's neck heated up. The last thing she wanted was to be alone with James Esh. What if he tried to kiss her again? "I'd really like to join the game," she replied. "If you're not wanting to play, maybe you can find something else to do until the ice cream has been made."

James reached under the table and squeezed Allison's hand. "I can't think of anything I'd rather do than spend time with you. So I guess if it means hittin' a *dumm* old ball around the bumpy grass, I'll be the first one in line."

Allison pulled her hand away and grabbed another piece of chicken. Maybe if she kept her mouth full of food she wouldn't be expected to make conversation.

❧

Aaron pushed a spoonful of macaroni salad around on his plate as irritation welled up in his soul like a gusher of water on a stormy day. He didn't like the way James Esh sat next to Allison, whispering in her ear like she was his girlfriend. Couldn't she see what he was up to? Didn't Allison realize all James wanted was a summer romance with no strings attached?

Isn't that all you *would consider where Allison is concerned?* Aaron clenched his fists. *If I'd come in my own buggy, and Joseph and Bessie had a way home, I'd head out now so I wouldn't have to watch James carry on like a lovesick cow.*

"You ain't eatin' much." Gabe leaned across the table and pointed at Aaron's plate. "If you're gonna beat me at croquet, then you'd better do something to build up your strength."

Aaron merely shrugged in response. He was in no mood for Gabe's jokes, and he wasn't sure he even wanted to get in on the game. Of course, if he didn't play, that would give James another chance to cozy up to Allison.

"You look like you're suckin' on a bunch of tart cherries," Gabe said. "Is there somethin' bothering you today?"

"Naw," Aaron lied. "I just ain't hungry."

"I'll bet he's savin' room for the ice cream we'll be having later on," Melinda said with a grin. She handed Aaron a dish of deviled eggs. "Would you like to try one of these?"

"No, thanks," he mumbled, pushing the plate away.

Gabe looked over at his wife and smiled. "Now that Melinda's eatin' for two, she takes second helpings of everything."

Melinda needled him in the ribs with her elbow. "That's not so and you know it."

Aaron's mouth fell open. "I—I didn't know you two were gonna have a *boppli*."

Melinda nodded, and Gabe's smile widened. "Should be born in October. I'm hopin' for a boy to help me in the woodworking shop."

"Well, congratulations."

"Danki. We're pretty excited about becoming parents," Gabe said.

Aaron grabbed his glass of iced tea and took a big drink. He could tell by his friend's cheerful expression that he was looking forward to becoming a daed. Aaron wondered what it would be like to have a loving wife and a boppli of his own. He cast a quick glance in Allison's direction. *If I were to marry, I'd want someone as sweet as her.*

❧

Allison did her best to avoid James as the women teamed up to play the first round of croquet against the men. Aunt Mary sat on the sidelines visiting with Katie's mother, Doris, and watching the children play a game of tag. Uncle Ben and Amos, Katie's father, had taken a walk to the barn.

There were extra balls and mallets, so each player had their own. Allison went first, since she was the guest of honor. Then it was Katie's turn, followed by Melinda, Sarah, and Katie's sister, Anna. Next, the men took turns.

"Sure is obvious that the fellows are tryin' to win this game," Melinda said to Allison when Gabe hit his ball through the middle wicket, leaving everyone else two wickets behind.

Allison wouldn't have admitted it, but she'd intentionally not played as well as she would have at home. She was trying to act like a woman and not a tomboy. "I guess it doesn't matter who wins, as long as everyone has fun," she said in response to Melinda's statement.

"That's true," Katie agreed. "And I'm having a real gut time."

"I didn't get much chance to visit with you at the last preaching service," Melinda said. "But I understand you're from Pennsylvania."

Allison nodded and took aim with her mallet. She gave the ball a light tap, but it missed the wicket by several inches.

"How long will you be in Webster County?" Melinda asked as Katie took her turn.

"Just 'til the end of summer."

"Do you like animals?" came the next question from Gabe's pretty, blond-haired wife.

"Some. I like dogs, although I've never had one as a pet."

"Really?"

"My aunt Catherine doesn't care much for pets," Allison explained.

"You'll have to go over to Melinda and Gabe's sometime," Katie said after she'd finished her turn. "Melinda's got more pets than you'll see at the zoo."

Allison's interest was piqued. She couldn't imagine having that many pets.

"I have an animal shelter where I care for orphaned animals or those that have been hurt and need a place to stay while they're recuperating," Melinda explained. "Gabe's a woodworker, and he's built me lots of cages to keep my critters in."

"Is that so?"

Melinda nodded, but it was Katie who spoke first. "Melinda used to work at the veterinary clinic in Seymour, so Dr. Franklin sends all his orphaned patients to her once he's done all he can for them."

"There must never be a dull moment at your place," Allison commented.

"That's for certain sure. I think my folks were real glad when I married Gabe and they no longer had to put up with all my animals and the crazy stunts they pulled." Melinda giggled. "Now it's Gabe's job to help me round up any runaway critters."

Allison thought the idea of having a safe haven for animals was wunderbaar. She figured Gabe Swartz must be a caring husband to have built cages for Melinda, not to mention him being willing to run after a bunch of stray animals.

"All right," Sarah shouted, interrupting the conversation. "Let's see if anyone can catch up with me now!"

Allison scanned the yard and was surprised to see her cousin's red ball lying a few feet from the final set of wickets. Apparently Sarah had made it through the previous four without her realizing it.

The women stood on the edge of the grass while the men took their turns, each with a determined look on his face. Aaron swung his mallet, and his ball ended up right next to Sarah's.

"This is gonna be a close game," Harvey shouted. "It's your turn, James, so do your best!"

James lined up his mallet, pulled both arms back, and let loose with a swing that sent the ball sailing through the air. Aaron was on his way to the sidelines when James's ball whacked him square in the knee.

Aaron crumpled to the ground with a muffled groan.

Allison rushed forward, but James caught her hand. "Don't worry about him; he's probably fakin' it."

"These balls are awfully hard, and I'm sure it hurts real bad," she said. By this time everyone had gathered around Aaron, and Allison couldn't see how he was doing.

"Aw, Aaron will be okay," James insisted. "A little ice on his knee and he'll be just fine."

Allison wasn't so sure about that. James had smacked his ball with a lot of force—enough to knock Aaron down. She pulled her hand free and started to move away, but James grabbed hold of her elbow and said, "Say, Allison, did you know there's to be another singing next Sunday night?"

She shook her head, wondering what the singing had to do with anything. Didn't James even care that he'd injured Aaron's knee?

"How would you like to take another ride home in my buggy?"

Allison opened her mouth to respond, but before she could get a word out, Aaron limped through the crowd and announced, "That won't be possible, because Allison is ridin' home with me!"

fourteen

Sitting on a bale of straw inside the Kauffmans' barn, Allison's stomach twisted like clothes being wrung in the washing machine. Even though the barbecue at her aunt and uncle's had been a whole week ago, her mind was still in a jumble over what had transpired during the game of croquet she and the other young people played after their meal. When Aaron announced that he would be taking her home after the singing the following Sunday night, it had taken her completely by surprise. Allison wondered if he'd said that to irritate James—or had he been trying to protect her from James's flirtatious ways?

It wasn't until after they'd finished eating their ice cream and everyone was getting ready to go home that Allison had been able to speak with Aaron alone. She closed her eyes and reflected on their conversation. . . .

ða.

"Can I have a word with you, Aaron?" Allison asked as Aaron hitched his horse to his open buggy.

Without turning, he merely nodded.

She licked her lips and searched for the right words. "I was wondering why you told James you'd be taking me home from the singing next week, and I'm curious about whether you meant it or not."

"Course I meant it."

"Mind if I ask why?"

He shrugged. "Didn't want to see you with James. He's trouble with a capital T."

Allison's heart sank clear to her toes. So it was only because Aaron was worried about James, not because he wanted to be alone with her. She should have known better than to get her hopes up.

"You don't have to protect me from James," she said sharply. "I'm perfectly capable of making my own decisions and speaking on my own behalf."

Aaron stared at her. "Are you saying you'd prefer to ride home with James after the singing?"

"I—I'm not saying that at all."

Aaron patted his horse's neck and went around to the driver's side of the buggy. "So, do you want a ride home after the singing or not?"

Common sense told Allison to reject Aaron's offer, in case he had only asked because he didn't like James, but another part of her wanted to be with him, so she smiled and nodded. "Jah, okay."

"See you next Sunday, if not before." Aaron climbed into the buggy, grabbed up the reins, and backed his horse away from the hitching post.

Allison turned toward the house, wondering why she felt so befuddled whenever she was in his presence.

❧

"Allison, did you hear what I just said?"

Allison's eyes popped open at the sound of Katie's sweet voice. Her friend stood beside her holding two glasses in her hands.

"Sorry. I was thinking about something," Allison mumbled.

"I thought maybe you'd fallen asleep." Katie giggled and handed one of the glasses to Allison. "Here's some cold root beer."

"Danki." Allison reached for the glass and took a sip. The frothy, refreshing soda tasted sweet and felt good on her parched lips. It was another warm evening, and summer was only beginning. She hated to think what the weather would be like by August.

"I'm surprised you're not sitting with Joseph," Allison commented as Katie took a seat beside her.

"Joseph isn't here yet, but Aaron showed up awhile ago. I figured you might be with him." Katie gave her a knowing look. "Since he's taking you home after the singing, I thought you might spend part of the evening together."

Allison shook her head. "Truth be told, I'm not sure Aaron even wants to take me home tonight."

"Are you kidding? Last week during our game of croquet he made it clear that was his intention."

"That's true, but I'm not convinced he made the announcement because he enjoys being with me."

Katie elbowed Allison gently in the ribs. "Puh! I can tell he likes you by the way he acts whenever you're around."

"What do you mean?"

"He carries on like a lovesick hundli."

Allison grunted. "Aaron's no puppy dog, and he's sure not in love with me. We barely know each other and haven't even been out together."

"Not yet. But tonight, with him taking you home from the singing, it will be your first date. This could be the start of many more dates for you and Aaron."

Allison's heart fluttered, and she willed herself to calm down. *It would be wunderbaar if Aaron wanted to court me during my time here for the summer. But that's probably not going to happen, so there's no use in me getting my hopes up for nothing.*

ﯤ

Ever since Aaron had arrived at the singing, he'd been hanging around the refreshment table trying to work up the nerve to take a plate of food over to Allison and visit with her awhile. A few minutes ago, he'd seen Katie Esh head over to the bale of straw where Allison sat, but he didn't feel right about interrupting their conversation. Besides, it wouldn't be good to give anyone the impression that they were a courting couple. It would be bad enough for them to be seen together when the evening ended and they left in his buggy. He'd probably have to take all kinds of ribbing from his friends—especially Gabe, who seemed to take pleasure in telling Aaron how great life was now that he was married to Melinda and they were expecting their first baby.

Aaron glanced across the room just in time to see James Esh swagger into the barn. His straw hat was tipped way back on his head, there was a red bandanna tied around his neck, and he wore a pair of blue jeans with holes in the knees. *Anything to draw attention to himself.*

After a quick survey of the room, James headed in the direction of Allison and Katie. Aaron clenched his fists and waited to see what would happen. Sure enough, James marched right up to Allison, bent over, and whispered something in her ear.

Aaron grabbed a handful of pretzels and inched his way closer to the bale of straw Allison and Katie shared.

Suddenly, Katie stood. She smiled at Allison, said something Aaron couldn't understand, and headed for the barn door. That's when Aaron noticed Joseph had arrived. Apparently, Katie cared more about being with his brother than she did protecting Allison from the likes of James Esh.

Katie had only been gone a few seconds when James plunked down next to Allison. She shifted on the bale of straw and pursed her lips. Aaron thought she looked uncomfortable, but he couldn't be certain what she was thinking.

He halted and leaned against one wall. At least he was close enough now that he might be able to hear what James said to her. *Should I go over there? Would Allison be irritated if I broke into their conversation, or would she appreciate the interruption?*

"I don't care what Aaron Zook said last Sunday," James said in a mocking tone. "When he announced that you'd be going home in his buggy tonight, he was only trying to get even with me for smacking him in the knee with the croquet ball."

Allison shook her head. "Aaron doesn't seem like the type of person to get even."

"Ha! How would you know what he's capable of doin'? You barely know the guy."

She turned and looked right at James. "I barely know you, either."

James chuckled. "That may be true, but I'd like to remedy that by takin' you home again tonight." He leaned closer, and

Aaron wondered if the fellow might try to kiss Allison right there in front of everyone.

Aaron held his breath and waited to hear what Allison would say next. After her comment the other day about being able to speak for herself, he didn't want to intervene unless it was necessary.

"I told you that I'm riding home with Aaron tonight," she said.

James grabbed hold of her arm and pulled her close to his side. "And I say you're ridin' with me."

That did it! With no thought of the consequences, Aaron marched over, seized James by the shirt collar, and pulled the man to his feet. "Excuse me, but I believe you're sittin' in my seat!"

Aaron didn't know who was more surprised—James, whose face was red as a tomato; Allison, whose eyes were huge as saucers; or himself. He'd never done anything quite so bold.

"Don't get yourself in a snit," James snarled. "I wasn't sayin' anything to Allison that she didn't wanna hear."

Aaron held his arms tightly against his sides. It was all he could do to keep from punching James right in the nose. "You're nothin' but trouble, and if I ever catch you bothering Allison again, I'll—"

"You'll what? Put my lights out?" James glared at Aaron like he was daring him to land the first punch.

"You know I won't fight you," Aaron mumbled. "But I can make trouble in other ways if you don't back off."

James took a step forward until he was nose to nose with Aaron. "What are you gonna do—run to the bishop or one of the ministers and tell 'em what a bad fellow I am?"

Aaron glanced around the room, feeling as if all eyes were on him. Sure enough, everyone within earshot was quietly watching him and James.

"Why don't you leave now, James? Knowin' the kind of things you usually do for entertainment, I'm sure an evening of singing and games would only bore you."

James looked down at Allison, who hadn't said one word since Aaron had arrived. "You want me to go?" he asked smoothly.

She nodded and stared at her hands, which were folded in her lap. "I think it would be best."

James lifted her chin with his thumb. "Okay, Allison Troyer. I'll head out on my own, but only because you asked so nicely." He threw Aaron an icy stare. "This ain't the end of it, ya know."

fifteen

Allison climbed into Aaron's buggy and settled herself in the front seat on the passenger's side. Even though she'd been alone with Aaron a few times before, she'd never felt as nervous as she did right now. She glanced at him as he stepped in and took the seat beside her. Their gazes met, and the moment seemed awkward. Was Aaron nervous, too? Would this be the only time he would offer her a ride home, or might he repeat the invitation?

Aaron gave her a brief smile and picked up the reins. "Mind if I trot the horse once we get on the main road?"

Allison shook her head. "Don't mind a'tall. The breezy air might help cool us off a bit."

"It has been a hot day," Aaron agreed. "We could use a good rain to lower the temperature some."

"I agree."

They pulled onto Highway C, and the buggy picked up speed when Aaron gave his horse the signal to trot.

"Ah, that feels better," Allison said as a puff of air lifted the strings of her kapp.

Aaron chuckled and pointed to his horse. "I think he's enjoyin' it, too."

"How's your sister doing?" Allison asked. "I heard she came home from the hospital early last week."

He nodded. "Emma's doin' real good, and we're thankful they got her into surgery before her appendix busted open."

Allison nodded. "That was a gut thing."

"Do you miss Pennsylvania much?" Aaron questioned, changing the subject.

"I miss Papa and my brothers." Allison figured it would be best not to mention that she didn't miss Aunt Catherine. It might make Aaron think she was *undankbaar*—ungrateful—to the woman who had taken her mother's place. *Aunt Catherine shouldn't be the one running Papa's house. That was my mamm's job, and God shouldn't have allowed her to die.*

"It won't be long before summer's over and you'll be on your way home," Aaron said, breaking into Allison's disconcerting thoughts.

"I hope I'm ready to go by August," she replied.

Aaron tipped his head and lifted one eyebrow in question.

"If I can't sew or cook well enough, it'll be hard to go home and face my daed. The only reason he sent me here was so Aunt Mary could teach me how to be a woman."

Aaron's cheeks turned red and he looked away. "I'd say you're already a woman."

Allison felt the heat of a blush stain her cheeks as well. She might look like a woman on the outside, but she had a long way to go before she would be ready to take on the responsibility of becoming a wife or a mother. Even if she did manage to accomplish that task, she would need to find a man who'd be willing to marry her.

"I've been wondering something," Aaron said, sounding hesitant.

"What's that?"

"It's about James Esh."

"What about him?"

"Are you interested in courting James?"

"What?" Allison's mouth dropped open.

"I said—"

"If I was interested in James, would I be riding home with you?"

"You rode home with him after the last singing."

"That's true."

A frown crushed Aaron's strong features. "James isn't right for you, Allison. He hasn't been baptized or joined the church, and even though he's in his twenties, he's still runnin' wild like some kid who's *ab im kopp*."

Allison felt a surge of guilt stab the core of her being. She hadn't been baptized or joined the church yet either. Did that mean she, too, was crazy? Her reluctance to join the church wasn't because she was going through rumspringa and wanted to experience things the modern world had to offer, however. It had more to do with her lack of faith in God.

They rode in silence the rest of the way home, and Allison was glad Aaron had dropped the subject of James Esh. It made her uncomfortable to think about the way James had carried on at the singing tonight.

When they pulled into Uncle Ben's driveway, Aaron stopped the buggy and came around to help Allison down. She had planned to step out on her own, but Aaron put his hands around her waist and lifted her out of the buggy like she weighed no more than a feather. He held her like that for several seconds, and Allison's heart pounded so hard she could hear it echoing in her ears. She remembered the unexpected kiss James had given her a few weeks ago. It hadn't been appreciated, but now. . . Allison shivered. If only she and Aaron were sweethearts. If he did decide to kiss her. . .

"I heard that your uncle's gonna rebuild his barn soon," Aaron said as he set Allison on the ground and took a step back. His ears were red, but she figured it could have been from the wind that had been blowing in their faces during the buggy ride.

Allison nodded, struggling to hide her disappointment. It was stupid to think he might offer her a kiss good night. "I believe Uncle Ben's planning to start on the barn sometime in the next few weeks."

"I imagine there'll be a work frolic then."

"Probably so."

"Most of the men in our community will be there to help." Aaron removed his straw hat and fanned his face with the brim. "Whew! Sure can't believe how hot it still is, even with the sun almost down."

"It will be hard to sleep tonight," she said, turning toward the house. "I wish I could sleep outside on the porch where it's not so stifling."

"You like sleepin' outdoors?" Aaron asked as he strode up the path beside her.

"I do. My friend Sally and I used to sleep on her front porch when we were younger. It was great fun to listen to the music of the crickets while we lay awake visiting and trying to count the stars."

"You remind me of my mamm," Aaron said as they stepped onto the porch. "She's always enjoyed the outdoors." He leaned on the porch railing as Allison moved toward the door.

Should I invite him in for a glass of cold milk and some cookies? No, he might think I was being too forward. Allison reached for the doorknob. "I appreciate the ride home. Danki."

"Maybe we can do it again sometime."

"I'd like that."

Aaron shuffled his feet across the wooden planks. "Well, good night, then."

"Good night, Aaron."

sixteen

Throughout the next several weeks, Allison kept busy helping her aunt and cousins in the garden, practicing her cooking skills, and making faceless dolls. Yet despite her busy days, thoughts of Aaron occupied her mind. Did he enjoy her company as much as she did his? Was he beginning to care for her, even a little bit? It had certainly seemed so on the Sunday night of the last singing, but she didn't want to get her hopes up.

"Your sewing abilities have improved," Aunt Mary commented as she stepped up to the treadle machine where Allison worked on a dark green dress for a faceless doll.

Allison looked up at her aunt and smiled. "I'd never be able to sew a straight seam if you hadn't been willing to work with me."

Aunt Mary placed a gentle hand on Allison's shoulder. "You've been a very gut student."

"Do you think I'm ready to sell some of these at the farmer's market?" Allison asked, motioning to the two dolls lying on one end of the sewing table.

"I believe so. In fact, Sarah and I plan to take some fresh produce to the market this Saturday. Would you like to share our table?"

"Jah, I surely would." Allison picked up the closest doll and studied its faceless form. Every time she looked at one of these dolls it reminded her that she felt faceless and would continue to feel that way until she figured out some way to get closer to God.

As though sensing Allison's troubled spirit, Aunt Mary pulled a chair over and sat down. "Is something bothering you, Allison? You look sad today."

Tears welled up in Allison's eyes, and she blinked, trying to dispel them. "Being with you and your family has made me realize there's something absent in my life."

"Are you missing your mamm? Is that the problem?"

Allison shrugged. "I don't remember her well enough to miss her, but I do miss having a mother."

Aunt Mary nodded. "That's understandable, but you had your aunt Catherine through most of your growing-up years, and now you have me." She patted Allison's hand. "I'm here for you whenever you need anything or just want to talk. And I hope you won't be too shy to ask."

Allison's throat felt clogged, and she wasn't sure she could speak. But there were things she wanted to say—questions she wished to ask. "I–I've never said this to anyone before, but I feel faceless, just like these dolls."

"What do you mean?"

"I don't know God personally, the way you seem to."

Aunt Mary smiled. "God is always there, Allison, if we just look for Him. Jeremiah 29:13 says, 'And ye shall seek me, and find me, when ye shall search for me with all your heart.' "

Allison pursed her lips. "How can I seek God when I don't feel as if He knows me?"

"Jeremiah 1:5 says: 'Before I formed thee in the belly I knew thee; and before thou camest forth out of the womb I sanctified thee.' " Her aunt smiled. "Isn't it wonderful to know that God knew us even before we were born?"

Allison could only nod in reply, wondering why no one had ever told her this before. Had she not been listening during the times she'd been in church, or had the ministers and bishop in her district never read those particular verses in any of their preaching services?

"God not only knew us before we were born," Aunt Mary went on to say, "but He loved us so much that He sent His Son Jesus to die for the sins of the world. By Christ's blood, God made a way for us to get to heaven. All we need to do is ask Him to forgive our sins and yield our lives to Him."

Allison had heard some of those things in church. She knew that Jesus was God's Son and had come to earth as a baby. When He grew up and became a man, He traveled around the country, teaching, preaching, and healing people of their diseases. Some men were jealous and plotted to have Jesus killed. She also knew the Bible made it clear that Jesus had died on a cross and was raised to life after three days. What she hadn't realized was that He had done it for the sins of the world—hers included.

She swallowed and drew in a shaky breath. "I—I sin every time I think or say something bad about Aunt Catherine. Even my anger toward God for taking my mamm away is a sin. He must be so disappointed in me."

Aunt Mary shook her head. "God loves you, Allison. You're His child, and He wants you to come to Him." She paused and squeezed Allison's hand. "Would you like to pray and ask God to forgive your sins? Would you like to invite Jesus into your heart right now?"

A shuddering sob escaped Allison's lips. "Jah, I would."

❧

When Aaron's mother stepped into the harness shop, he looked up from his work at the riveting machine. A strand of brown hair had come loose from her bun, and there were dark circles under her eyes. She looked tired. Probably had spent another night helping Grandma take care of Grandpa Raber, whose arthritis seemed to be getting worse all the time.

"What brings you out to the harness shop?" he asked. "Paul's not here. He went into town for some supplies."

"I know he did." Aaron's mother moved closer to him. "I was supposed to go over to Leah Swartz's this morning to work on a quilt with her and a couple other women. But since neither Grandma nor Grandpa are feeling well, I didn't want to leave Bessie alone to care for them and Emma, too."

"But Emma's doin' better, isn't she?" Aaron knew his mother didn't get away much anymore, and he figured it would do her good to spend the day with Gabe's mamm and whoever else would attend the quilting bee.

"Jah, but she still tires easily, and I like to keep a close eye on her."

"Can't you take Emma with you?"

"I don't think she's up to a whole day out yet." His mother glanced around the room. "Since you have no customers at the moment, I was hopin' you might run over to Leah's and let her know I won't be comin' after all."

Aaron chewed on the inside of his cheek as he contemplated her request. "Paul won't like it if he gets back from Seymour and finds the shop closed. Can't you send Davey or Zachary?"

"I could, but they aren't home. Zachary's helping Joseph at the tree farm today, and Davey went fishing with his friend, Samuel Esh."

Just the mention of the name *Esh* set Aaron's teeth on edge. Samuel was James's younger brother, and Aaron worried that the boy might follow in his unruly brother's footsteps. "Might not be a good idea for Davey to be hangin' around Samuel," he muttered.

Mom's dark eyebrows drew together. "Why would you say something like that?"

He shrugged. "Samuel's brother James is nothin' but trouble. If Samuel goes down the same path, he could lead Davey astray."

"For a boy of only fourteen, your youngest brother has a good head on his shoulders. I don't think he'd be easily swayed, even if Samuel suggests they do something wrong."

"I hope you're right, but no one, not even my levelheaded little brother, is exempt from trouble if it comes knockin' at the right moment." Aaron was so upset about the idea of Davey hanging around Samuel that he felt tempted to chomp off the end of a fingernail. Instead, he reached for another hunk of leather and positioned it under the riveter.

His mother frowned. "You seem distressed, and I have a feeling it goes deeper than your concern for Davey."

"Maybe so."

"Would you like to talk about it?"

He merely shrugged in response.

"Does it involve Allison Troyer?"

"What?" Aaron nearly dropped the piece of leather, but he rescued it before it hit the floor. "Why would ya think that?"

His mother pulled a wooden stool over to the machine and took a seat. "I heard that you escorted Allison home from the last singing."

"Joseph's a *blappermaul*," Aaron grumbled. "He ought to keep quiet about things that are none of his business." And he would be sure to remind his blabbermouth brother about that later.

"Your brother did mention what happened at the singing, but you've been acting strange ever since Allison arrived in Webster County."

Aaron's only reply was a frustrated grunt.

"Are you planning to court her?"

"Haven't decided that yet."

"She seems like a nice girl, and since you've never had a steady girlfriend—"

"There wouldn't be much point in me goin' steady," Aaron interrupted. "It would make a girl believe I might ask her to marry me someday."

His mother nodded. "That is usually the case."

"Well, I ain't gettin' married. Plain and simple."

Mom clucked her tongue. "You've been saying that since you were little, but I figured once you found the right girl you'd decide to settle down and start a family of your own."

"Nope."

"Mind if I ask why?"

The truth was, Aaron did mind. He didn't want to talk about the one thing that had troubled him ever since his real daed died. But he knew if he didn't offer some sort of explanation, his mamm would keep plying him with questions.

"I—uh—haven't found anyone who'd be willin' to work in the harness shop with me," he mumbled.

"Puh! There's a lot more to marriage than workin' side by side on harnesses five or six days a week." Mom pursed her lips. "Paul and I still have a gut marriage, and I'm not helping here anymore."

Aaron tried to focus on the piece of leather he'd been punching holes in, but it was hard to concentrate when his mamm sat beside him, saying things he'd rather not hear.

"Does the idea of marriage scare you, Aaron? Is that why you're shying from it?"

He looked up and met her gaze. Did she know what he was thinking? Could Mom sense his fear? "I'm scared of fallin' in love, gettin' married, and then havin' my wife snatched away from me the way Dad was from you!" he blurted.

Mom's mouth dropped open; then she quickly reached out and touched his arm. "Oh, Aaron, I'm sorry we've never talked about this before. I can see by your pained expression that you're deeply disturbed."

Aaron opened his mouth to respond, but his mother rushed on. "Life is full of disappointments, son, but we have to take some risks. None of us can predict the future, for only God knows what's to come."

"If you had known Dad's buggy would be hit by a car and that you'd be left to raise four boys on your own, would you still have married him?"

She nodded as tears filled her dark eyes. "I wouldn't give up a single moment of the time I had with your daed."

"You really mean that?"

"I do. And look how God has blessed me," his mamm said with feeling. "I found a wonderful husband in Paul, and I have four terrific sons and two sweet daughters. As much as it hurt when I lost your daed, I've had the joy of finding love again."

Aaron drew in a deep breath. Was it possible that he could set his fears aside and find the same kind of happiness Mom had found? Was Allison the woman he might find it with?

seventeen

Allison had just placed her faceless dolls on the table Aunt Mary had set up for them at the farmer's market when she caught sight of Aaron heading her way. Her heart lurched. Would he be as happy to see her as she was to see him?

"I didn't know you were going to be here today," he said, stopping in front of the table and leaning on the edge of it.

"I didn't expect to see you either. I figured you would be working at the harness shop."

"I usually do work on Saturdays, but Paul said I could have the day off." Aaron grinned. "I can't figure out why, but lately he's sure been nice to me."

"Maybe he appreciates all the hard work you did at the shop while he and your mamm were in Springfield during your sister's hospital stay."

"That could be." He glanced around. "Are you here alone?"

She shook her head. "Aunt Mary and Sarah are getting some produce and baked goods from the buggy. I'll be sharing this table with them."

Aaron pointed to one of Allison's dolls. "Looks like you've been hard at work. Those are real nice."

"Danki. It took me awhile, but I think I'm finally getting the feel for the treadle machine."

He nodded. "I would say so."

"Are you planning to sell anything today, or did you just come to look around?" she asked.

"I came to see my friend, Gabe. He's supposed to be selling some of his wooden items here today. Melinda will probably sell her drawings and maybe some of her grandpa's homemade jam."

"I didn't know Melinda was an artist," Allison said with interest. "With all her animals to care for, plus keeping house and

102

cooking for a husband, I wonder how she finds time to draw."

"Melinda makes time to do whatever she feels is important."

"Maybe she won't be able to do so much once the boppli is born."

Aaron chuckled. "Knowing Melinda, she'll try to do everything she's doin' now, and then some."

"Aunt Mary's kind of like that," Allison said. "She keeps busy all the time and is good at everything she does."

Aaron picked up one of the faceless dolls. "Looks to me like you're able to do lots of things, too."

Allison shook her head. "I'm good at baseball, fishing, and most outdoor chores; but my sewing skills are just average, and I still can't cook very well." She grimaced. "You should have tasted the buttermilk biscuits I made the other night. They were chewy like leather."

He snickered. "I doubt they were that bad."

"Let's just say, nobody had seconds."

He placed the doll back on the table. "Speaking of food. . . How'd ya like to go across the street with me at noon and have a juicy burger at the fast-food restaurant?"

Allison nodded. "I'd like that." She couldn't get over how friendly Aaron seemed to be. All the times she'd been with him before, he'd seemed kind of nervous and hesitant, like he might be holding back from something. But the way Aaron looked at Allison now made her feel like he really wanted to be with her.

"Guess I'll head over to Gabe's table, but I'll be back to pick you up for lunch a little before noon."

"I'll be looking forward to it."

&

As Aaron headed across the parking lot, he thought about his conversation with Allison. He couldn't get over how peaceful and sweet she looked this morning. He wondered if something had happened since he'd last seen her. Maybe she was just excited about being at the farmer's market and trying to sell some of her dolls.

A few minutes later, Aaron spotted Gabe and Melinda's table on the other side of the open field. He jogged over to it and tapped his friend on the shoulder. "Hey, how's it going?"

Gabe nodded at his wife. "Why don't you ask her? She's the one who seems to be selling everything this morning."

Melinda smiled. "Most people have been buying Grandpa's rhubarb-strawberry jam, but I have sold a couple of my drawings."

"At least you've got people coming over to your table," Aaron said.

"How come you're not workin' today?" Gabe asked.

"Paul gave me the day off, and since I knew you were planning to be at the market, I figured I'd come by and see you."

"Anything in particular you wanted to see me about?"

Aaron placed his hands on the table and leaned closer to Gabe. "I was wonderin' if I could hire you to do a job for me."

Gabe's eyebrows lifted. "What kind of job would you want to hire me for?"

"I need a dog run built for Rufus. He's not happy being chained up all the time, and if I let him run free, he chases Bessie's kittens."

"That can be a problem," Gabe agreed.

"You're right. Remember when Gabe built a dog run for my brother's dog?" Melinda put in. "Jericho was chasing my animals all over the place, and he kept breaking free from his chain."

Aaron nodded. "Gabe did a good job on it, which is why I thought of hiring him to build a run for Rufus. I'll pay whatever it costs," he added with a nod.

"Sorry, but you can't hire me," Gabe said.

"How come? Are you too busy at your woodworking shop?"

"No, but you're my friend, Aaron. I'll gladly build the dog run, but it'll be as a favor, with no money involved."

"That's nice of you," Aaron said with gratitude. "I'll pay for all the supplies, of course."

"Sounds fine. When do you want me to start?"

"Whenever you have the time. There's no rush, but the sooner I get Rufus off that chain, the sooner Bessie will quit buggin' me."

Gabe chuckled. "I'll come over and take a look at it some evening after work. How's that sound?"

Aaron scratched the side of his head. "Say, I've got an idea. Why don't you and Melinda join Allison and me for some fishing at the Rabers' pond one night next week? If you drop by my place before we go, I can show you where I was thinkin' the dog run could be built."

Melinda spoke up before Gabe could open his mouth. "I think that would be fun. I love going to the pond, where there's so much wildlife. And it would give me a chance to get to know Allison better."

"It's a date, then." Aaron's face heated up. "I do still need to ask Allison, but I'm pretty sure she'll say yes."

Gabe shook his head as he gazed up at the trees. "I knew you had more than a casual interest in that woman."

❧

Allison sat in a booth at the restaurant, with Aaron in the seat across from her. They both had double cheeseburgers and an order of french fries in front of them. This felt like a real date, and she couldn't seem to calm her racing heart. Was it her imagination, or did the look of admiration on Aaron's face mean he was beginning to care for her? Maybe he didn't mind that she was a tomboy. Maybe he was glad she was like his mother in some ways. Oh, she hoped that was the case. And she hoped. . . What was she hoping for? That she could stay in Webster County? Was that what she wanted to do?

As Allison bit into another fry, she tried to imagine what it would be like if she and Aaron were married. *Would he be willing to teach me how to work in the harness shop? I'll never find out if Aaron and I can have a future together if I go back to Pennsylvania at the end of summer. If Aaron asked me to stay, I would write Papa a letter and see what he thought of the idea.*

"There's something about you that looks different today," Aaron said, breaking into Allison's thoughts.

She smiled. "Actually, I am different."

"In what way?"

"I accepted Jesus as my Savior last week."

His forehead wrinkled. "You've never done that before?"

She shook her head. "I'd heard some of our ministers talk about God's Son and how Jesus was crucified on the cross, but until Aunt Mary explained things to me, I didn't realize He had died for my sins."

"I suppose there are some in our community who don't understand about having a personal relationship with Christ," Aaron said. "But my mamm started reading the Bible to me, my brothers, and sisters as soon as we were old enough to comprehend things. I confessed my sins when I was fifteen and joined the church by the time I was eighteen." He reached for his glass of root beer. "Of course that don't mean I'm the perfect Christian, and I've had my share of problems along the way."

"I doubt there's anyone in this world who hasn't had problems," Allison said. "But with Jesus living in my heart, I feel like I'll be able to deal with anything that comes my way."

He smiled. "That's where Bible reading and prayer comes in. I'm trying to remember to do both every day."

"Me, too. It's the only way to stay close to God." She blotted her lips with the paper napkin. "I used to feel like the dolls I make—faceless and without a purpose. Now that I know God in a personal way, I think my purpose in life is to share His love through my actions as well as my words."

It seemed as though Aaron wanted to say something more, but they were interrupted when Gabe and Melinda walked up to their table.

"It looks like you two are about done eating," Gabe said, thumping Aaron on the shoulder.

"Just about."

"Mind if we join you?"

Aaron looked at Allison, like he was waiting for her

approval. When she nodded and slid over, he said, "Sure, have a seat."

Melinda slipped in beside Allison, and Gabe plunked down next to Aaron. "What'd Allison say about going fishin'?" he asked, reaching over and grabbing one of Aaron's french fries.

Aaron's ears turned red, and he looked almost guilty. "I—uh—haven't asked her yet."

"The guys want to take us fishing some night this week," Melinda said before either Aaron or Gabe could explain. "I hope you can go, because I'd like the chance to get better acquainted with you."

"I plan to take my canoe along," Aaron said quickly. "Haven't had the chance to use it yet this summer."

Allison smiled. While she knew that she needed to cook and sew in order to hopefully become a wife someday, she was glad that Aaron didn't mind if she did some tomboy things, too. "That sounds like fun. Jah, I'd really like to go."

eighteen

Excitement welled up in Allison's soul as Aaron and Gabe lifted the canoe from the back of the market wagon he had driven to the pond. It would be fun to sit in the boat and fish in the deepest part of the pond rather than trying to do it from shore.

"Sure is a beautiful evening," Melinda commented.

Allison nodded.

Melinda spread a quilt on the ground and motioned Allison to come over. "Would you like to have a seat so we can visit while the men get the canoe into the water and get our fishing gear ready to use?"

"Sure." Allison dropped to the quilt, and Melinda did the same.

"Oh, look, there's a little squirrel over by that tree," Melinda said excitedly.

"You really like animals, don't you?" Allison asked.

"Jah, almost as much as Aaron likes you," Melinda replied with a wink.

"What?"

"I've seen the way he looks at you. And Gabe tells me Aaron has given up his nasty habit of biting off his nails." Melinda clucked her tongue. "A change like that could only come about for one reason. He wants to impress someone—namely, you."

The back of Allison's neck radiated with heat, and she knew it wasn't from the warmth of the evening sun. "Has Aaron told Gabe he has an interest in me?"

Melinda shrugged. "I don't know about that, but I do know Aaron has never shown much interest in any woman until you came along."

Allison shifted on the quilt, tucking her legs under her long blue dress. "Even if Aaron does care for me, I'll be leaving at the end of summer."

"You can always write to each other."

"I suppose we could, but it would be hard to develop a lasting relationship with me living in Pennsylvania and him living here."

"I guess that depends on how you feel about Aaron," Melinda said. "Are you as smitten with him as he seems to be with you?"

Allison felt the warmth on her neck spread quickly to her face. "I—I do think he's cute, and he is fun to be with."

"Has he kissed you yet?"

Allison's eyebrows lifted. "Of course not. We don't know each other well enough for that." She thought about James's kiss, but that hadn't been mutual.

Melinda sighed and leaned back on her elbows. "If I live to be one hundred, I'll always remember the first time Gabe kissed me."

"Oh?"

"We'd had several dates, but whenever it seemed as if Gabe was about to kiss me, someone or something interrupted us." Melinda chuckled. "Poor Gabe. I think he was about to give up. But then the night of my nineteenth birthday came, and we finally had our first kiss."

Allison tried to imagine what it would feel like to have Aaron's arms around her, with his lips touching hers in a romantic embrace.

"Who's ready for the first canoe ride?" Gabe called.

Allison shielded her eyes from the sun filtering through the trees and realized that the canoe was already in the water.

"Why don't you go ahead?" Melinda suggested. "I'd like to draw awhile, and Gabe can fish from shore while he keeps me company."

Since Allison knew that Aaron didn't think it was unladylike for her to fish, she didn't need any coaxing. She scrambled to her feet and started for the pond.

"Wait a minute!" Melinda called. She rushed over to Allison and handed her a couple of large safety pins.

"What are these for?"

"To pin your skirt between your legs."

Allison tipped her head in question. "Why would I want to do that?"

"In case the canoe tips over and you end up going for a swim you hadn't planned on." Melinda smiled. "My aunt Susie, who recently got married and moved to a small Amish community in Montana, showed me how to do that when we were young girls."

"I don't plan on moving around much in the canoe, so I doubt it will tip over."

"Even so, it never hurts to be prepared."

Allison shrugged and took the pins. She bent over and attached them to the inside of her dress, laughing as she did so. "I guess this is the Amish version of trousers for women."

Melinda nodded. "Jah. It's real fashionable, don't ya think?"

"Sure is." Allison wondered what Aaron would think of her getup, but she decided not to worry about it and just try to have fun. She trotted off toward the pond, and when she reached the canoe, she grabbed Aaron's hand and stepped carefully in.

Aaron's gaze went to her safety-pinned skirt, but he never said a word. He just grabbed up a paddle, hollered for Gabe to let go of the canoe, and propelled them toward the middle of the pond.

&

It had been hard for Aaron not to laugh when Allison got into the canoe with her dress pinned between her knees, but he wasn't about to say anything. She might take it wrong, and he didn't want anything to ruin their evening together.

When they reached the middle of the pond, they baited their hooks, cast their lines into the water, and sat in companionable silence for a time. It was peaceful with the ripple of water lapping the sides of the canoe and the warble of birds serenading them from the nearby trees.

I could get used to being with this woman, Aaron thought as he watched Allison lean her head back and close her eyes. *Can I really set my fears about marriage aside and try to build a relationship with her? I want to. In fact, I've never wanted anything so much or felt so happy as when I'm with her.* He grimaced. *But she'll be leaving for Pennsylvania in a few months, and then what?*

Aaron cleared his throat, and Allison's eyes popped open. "What's wrong? Have you got a nibble?" she asked, glancing at the end of his pole.

"Nope. I just wanted to ask you something."

"What is it?"

"I was wondering. . . ." Aaron fought the temptation to bite off a fingernail. Why did he feel so tongue-tied when all he wanted to do was to ask her a simple question?

"What were you wondering?" she prompted.

He drew in a deep breath, hoping it would give him the courage to say what was on his mind. "I enjoy your company and would like to court you, Allison. I was hopin' you might consider staying on here longer instead of leaving in August like you'd planned."

Allison's eyes glowed with a look of happiness. "To tell you the truth, I had been thinking about writing my daed and asking if he would mind if I stayed here a few more months."

"Really? You've been planning to do that?"

"Jah. And I'm pleased that you want to court me, because I enjoy being with you." She smiled at Aaron so sweetly he knew he had to kiss her right then.

As he leaned toward Allison the canoe rocked gently, so he grabbed both sides, hoping to hold it steady. When it settled, he inched forward until his lips were inches from hers. Allison made no move to resist, and he breathed a sigh of relief. Maybe she wanted the kiss as much as he did.

Aaron extended his arms and reached for Allison, but before he could get his hands around her waist, the boat began to vibrate. He tried to steady it, but there wasn't time. In one quick movement, the canoe rolled over, and *splash*—they were plunged into the chilly water.

nineteen

Aaron took in a noseful of water as he dove under for the third time, frantically searching for Allison. Where was she, and why hadn't she surfaced when he did? Could she have hit her head on a rock and been knocked unconscious? No, the water level was too deep in the middle of the pond. It wasn't likely that she could have gone under that far.

The water in the pond was awful murky, and Aaron couldn't see much at all. He surfaced again and gulped in a breath of air. Treading water, he scanned the area around the canoe, which was turned upside down and bobbed like a cork. "Allison! Where are you, *hatzli*—sweetheart?"

He heard Melinda's terrified shouts from shore, and then water splashing. Aaron was glad to see Gabe swimming toward him. "I can't find Allison! You've gotta help me find her," he shouted.

Gabe had just reached the canoe when one side of it lifted, and Allison popped her head out. "What's all the yelling about?"

"Thank the Lord you're okay," Aaron hollered as relief flooded his soul. "I was afraid you had drowned."

She shook her head. "I had all the air I needed under the canoe."

"Do you know how to swim?" Gabe asked her.

"Of course I do. I'm able to tread water, too."

Aaron held the edge of the canoe while Allison swam out. "Let's get this thing turned over," he called to Gabe.

"Right!" Gabe grabbed hold, and they lifted it together. A few seconds later, the canoe was in an upright position again.

"We'll hold it steady while you climb in," Aaron instructed, nodding at Allison.

"I might be safer out here," she said in a teasing voice. "Besides, the cool water feels kind of good."

"You'd better do as Aaron says," Gabe put in, "or we'll be here all day arguing with him."

"Oh, okay, but please don't let go of the canoe. I've already had one drink of pond water, and it's all I need for the day."

Gabe steadied the canoe with both hands, while Aaron held on with one hand. The other hand he used to give Allison a boost. When she was safely inside, he handed her the paddle, which he'd found floating nearby. "Think you can row this back to shore?" he asked.

"I'm sure I can, but what about you? And what about our fishing gear?"

Aaron glanced at the shadowy water. "I'm afraid it's at the bottom of the pond, but that's not important. I'm just relieved that you're all right."

"I'm glad you're okay, too."

"Gabe and I will swim alongside of you. I don't want to chance tippin' the canoe again by me trying to climb in."

Allison looked like she might argue the point, but Gabe intervened once more. "Aaron's right. You'll do better on your own, and we're both good swimmers. We can help steady the boat if you run into a problem."

"Okay." Allison grabbed the paddle and soon had the canoe gliding toward land.

Aaron was tired when they finally got there, but he was thankful the accident had happened while they were in a small pond and not in a larger body of water. He and Gabe pushed the canoe onto shore, and Melinda came running as soon as Allison climbed out. "That was so scary!" she exclaimed. "I'm glad everyone's okay."

"Just sopping wet." Allison grabbed the edge of her dress and wrung out the excess water. "I must look a mess."

Aaron gazed at her, feeling affection well up in his chest. Any other woman would have probably cried or complained about her plight, but not Allison. There she stood, her dress completely soaked. Her hair had come loose from its bun, spilling from her white kapp, which hung down her back by the narrow strips of material tied under her chin. Yet she was a good sport and had even been able to laugh about it. At that moment, Aaron knew he had fallen hopelessly in love with Allison Troyer.

ॐ

Allison shivered as a chill ran through her body, but she didn't utter a word of complaint. Aaron had almost kissed her, and if the canoe hadn't capsized, she was sure he would have.

Melinda draped a quilt around Allison's shoulders. "I think we should go, Gabe," she said, glancing at her husband. "The three of you need to get out of those wet clothes."

"I'll be okay if I sit in the sun awhile," Allison argued.

"What sun?" Aaron pointed to the clouds overhead. "Looks like our sun is gone, and rain might be on the way."

"Well, we can't get any wetter than we are," Gabe said with a chuckle.

"Except for me," Melinda reminded.

Gabe shook his head, sending a spray of water all over her navy blue dress. "Now everyone's wet."

Melinda planted both hands on her ever-widening hips and scowled at him, but Allison could see by the twinkle in Melinda's eyes that she wasn't really upset by her husband's antics. "Just for that, I'm going to yodel all the way home," Melinda announced.

"Go ahead. I'm not Grandpa Stutzman; I like it whenever you yodel."

"Oh, yeah? Well, see if you like this." Melinda cupped her hands around her mouth and let loose with a terrible shriek. "Oh-lee-oh-lee-oh-lee-de-tee!" She held the last note and made it go so high that Gabe finally covered his ears. Allison and Aaron did the same.

"Enough already! I'm sorry I got water on your dress," Gabe apologized.

Allison laughed and Aaron reached for her hand. "Now

that's true love, wouldn't ya say?"

She gazed at his handsome face, still dripping with pond water. *What I'm feeling for you—that's true love.*

⁂

On Saturday morning, Allison awoke to hammers pounding against wood and the deep murmur of men's voices. She climbed out of bed and rushed over to the window, then pulled the dark curtain aside. There were at least a dozen men in the yard, moving back and forth from the barn to the plywood-covered sawhorses where all their supplies were laid out. She'd forgotten today was Saturday and they would be tearing down Uncle Ben's rickety old barn. Next week, if everything went well, construction on the new barn would begin.

Allison hurried to get washed and dressed. She knew Aunt Mary needed her more than ever today, as it would be the women's job to feed the men and see that they had plenty of water and snacks to sustain them throughout the day.

I wonder if Aaron will be able to get off work so he can help today. Allison thought about his parting words when he'd brought her home from their evening at the pond two nights ago.

"I hope our unexpected swim didn't ruin things between us," Aaron had said in a serious tone.

"Of course not. I thought it was kind of exciting," she'd replied.

Allison had hoped Aaron might kiss her good-bye, but when her cousin Harvey showed up wanting to know why they were both so wet, she knew the kiss wouldn't happen. She could still see Aaron's handsome face smiling at her before he drove away in his buggy. It made her even more anxious to see him again.

Allison entered the kitchen and found Aunt Mary and Sarah bustling around. "Sorry I'm late," she apologized. "Until I woke up to all that pounding, I'd forgotten the men would begin tearing down the old barn today."

Aunt Mary smiled. "That's all right. You're here now, and we can certainly use another pair of hands."

"What would you like me to do?"

"The menfolk have had their breakfast already, so if you'd like to fix yourself something to eat, you can make a batch of gingerbread when you're done."

Allison wished she could do something that had nothing to do with food, but she nodded agreeably and headed for the refrigerator to get some milk.

"Want me to see if the mail's here yet?" Sarah asked her mother.

"That would be fine." Aunt Mary nodded at some envelopes lying on the table. "Put those bills in the box for the mailman to pick up, would you, please?"

"Sure." Sarah grabbed the mail off the table and was almost to the door when Allison remembered the letter she had written to Papa the night before.

"I've got a letter that needs to go out," she said. "Would you wait a minute while I run upstairs and get it?"

Sarah's only reply was a quick nod.

"Did you write your daed a letter?" Aunt Mary asked.

"Jah. I've asked him if he would mind if I stay on here awhile after summer's over, and I told him you said it was okay."

Her aunt smiled. "I hope he agrees."

Allison nodded. "Me, too."

❧

As Aaron pulled his buggy into the Kings' yard, he noticed Gabe's rig in front of him. They both pulled up to the hitching rail near the corral and unhooked their horses from the buggies.

"I was going to start work on Rufus's dog run today," Gabe said. "But I figured I was needed more here."

"That's okay. Rufus has waited this long, so a little longer won't matter." Aaron led his horse to the corral, and Gabe followed.

"From the looks of all the men milling around the yard, I'd say every Amish shop in Webster County must be closed for the day," Gabe commented.

Aaron nodded. "Paul didn't think twice about closin' up the harness shop. He should be along shortly, I expect."

Gabe pointed across the yard. "I think my daed's here already."

"Guess we'd better go see what jobs we're needed to do."

"I expect you're right."

Sometime later, while Aaron was hauling a stack of wood from the old barn to the pile across the yard, he spotted Allison heading that way. She smiled and waved, and since his hands were full, he nodded.

"I was wondering if you'd be here today," she said when she caught up to him.

"Wouldn't have missed it." He winked at her. "I've been lookin' forward to seeing how you look in dry clothes."

Allison's cheeks turned crimson. "Aaron Zook, are you flirting with me?"

He dropped the wood onto the growing pile and grinned. "Maybe so."

"I wrote a letter to my daed last night, and it's in the mailbox right now."

"Oh?"

"I asked if he would mind if I stayed here awhile past August."

He frowned. "Just awhile?"

Her blush deepened. "Well, as long as Aunt Mary and Uncle Ben are willing to put up with me. How's that sound?"

Aaron took a step toward her. It was all he could do to keep from pulling her into his arms and kissing her upturned mouth. "I'm glad to hear that, and I hope your daed says you can stay on indefinitely."

"We'll have to see about that." Allison motioned to what remained of the barn. "I wish I could help the menfolk tear the wood off the walls instead of serving them cold drinks and the lunch I'll be helping prepare."

He chuckled and shook his head. "Now why would someone as pretty as you want to get her hands all dirty?"

She slapped his arm playfully. "Are you teasin' me?"

"Jah." The truth was, Aaron was impressed with Allison's willingness to help the men; and if he had his way, she'd be working alongside of him all day. But he was pretty sure her uncle would never go for that. Except for Paul, most Amish men he knew thought a woman's place was in the kitchen.

Allison released a sigh. "I suppose I should get back inside. I've got two loaves of gingerbread baking, and if I'm not careful, they'll be overdone."

"I'll be lookin' forward to sampling a piece," Aaron said as he took a couple of steps toward the work site. Suddenly, he turned back around. "Say, how'd you like to go over to Katie Esh's place and pick strawberries with me one evening next week? Katie's mamm told my mamm that the berries are comin' to an end, and if we don't get 'em soon, they'll all be gone."

Allison smiled. "I'd like that. Katie had mentioned the idea to me several weeks ago, and I haven't made the time yet."

Aaron reached under his straw hat and scratched the side of his head. "Guess I'd better ask my brother Joseph to join us. He and Katie are crazy about each other, and this could be like a double date."

"That sounds gut to me." Allison flashed him another smile and headed for the house.

Aaron started toward the old barn as he hummed a song they sometimes sang at their singings. He thought about the words and how they related to the way he felt about Allison. "Every minute of the day I'm thinkin' 'bout you; and without you, life is just a crazy dream. Every breath I take I'm hopin' that you're hopin' that I'm hopin' you'll stay here with me."

twenty

"I'm glad we're finally getting to do this," Katie said as Allison climbed down from her uncle's buggy.

"Me, too. I love ripe, juicy strawberries, and Aunt Mary said if I bring enough home she'll teach me to make strawberry pie."

"I'm sure there'll be plenty for that." Katie pointed to the garden, where clusters of fat strawberries grew in abundance. "I was surprised to see you drive in alone. I figured Aaron and Joseph would stop off at your place on the way over and give you a ride."

Allison shook her head. "When I saw Aaron on Sunday, I told him I would drive myself, since I knew he'd be working at the harness shop 'til suppertime and Joseph would be doing the same at the Christmas tree farm." She glanced at the road in front of the Eshes' place. "I hope they get here soon."

Katie grinned and her cheeks turned pink. "Jah. I always look forward to spending time with Joseph."

Allison's heart hammered with excitement. She hoped what she felt for Aaron wasn't just a silly crush.

"We don't have to wait until the fellows arrive to start pickin'," Katie said, shielding her eyes from the evening sun filtering through the trees. "I can run into the house and get some containers right now."

"That's fine with me," Allison replied. "The sooner I get started, the more berries I'll have to take home to Aunt Mary."

Katie smiled and hurried off.

Allison strolled around the edge of the garden, breathing in the pungent aroma of dill weed and feasting her eyes on the colorful vegetables growing among a few scattered weeds. In addition to the strawberries, there were all kinds of produce that would soon be ready for harvest—plump burgundy beets, long skinny pole beans, ginger-colored carrots with leafy, green tops, an abundance of tomatoes, and lots of squash.

She bent down and plucked a fat, red berry off the vine, then popped it into her mouth. "Umm. . .this is wunderbaar." She swished the juice around on her tongue, savoring the succulent sweetness and allowing it to trickle down her throat.

Allison heard the screen door slam shut, and she glanced up at the house. Katie stepped onto the back porch, holding two plastic containers. When she reached the berry patch, she handed one to Allison. "I see someone's been sampling the goods already," she said with a chuckle. "There's berry juice on your chin."

Allison rubbed the spot Katie had pointed to and laughed. "Jah, I'm guilty."

"Shall we start pickin'?"

"Sure." Allison knelt at the end of the first row, and Katie took the next row over.

"Maybe we can get our containers filled before Aaron and Joseph show up," Katie said.

"Might could be." Allison plucked off several berries and placed them in her container, being careful not to crush any. "I haven't seen your cousin James lately," she commented. "He wasn't at church last week, and he didn't come to help tear down Uncle Ben's barn on Saturday." James had been on Allison's mind ever since she'd made things right with God, because she knew he needed a personal relationship with the heavenly Father, too. He seemed angry and brash, thinking only of himself. God could change anyone's heart, and Allison knew it was not His will that any should perish.

"James doesn't care much for church these days, and he doesn't worry about helping anyone. He probably hired a driver or hitchhiked his way to Springfield for the day so he could have some fun." Katie scrunched up her nose. "I'm surprised that rowdy cousin of mine hasn't bought himself a car by now, the way some Amish men do when they're goin' through rumspringa."

"Maybe James is away on a trip. That might be why he hasn't been around."

"Could be. Never know what the unpredictable man might be up to."

Allison looked up when she heard a horse's hooves clomping against the pavement. Her heartbeat matched the rhythmic sound, and she hoped it was Aaron and Joseph's buggy coming up the road. Sure enough, Aaron's open black buggy slowed at the end of the driveway and made a sharp turn onto the Eshes' property.

"They're here!" Katie scrambled to her feet and rushed over to the hitching rail near her father's barn. Allison followed.

"Sorry we're late," Aaron apologized as he and Joseph jumped down from the buggy. "Paul and I had a harness that needed fixing while the customer waited, and we were late for supper."

"That's okay. You're here now." Katie gave Joseph a deep-dimpled smile.

"Would you rather I hitch my horse to the rail or put him in the corral?" Aaron asked her.

"Whatever you want is fine. My daed's still out in the fields with my brother Elam, so none of the workhorses are in the corral yet."

"We'll meet you in the garden when we get the horse unhitched," Joseph said.

Aaron waved his brother aside. "You go on ahead. I don't need any help."

"Let's go then." Joseph reached for Katie's hand, and Allison followed as the happy couple hurried toward the berry patch.

Soon Katie and Joseph were on their knees together, and Allison returned to the spot she'd been working on before the men showed up. Rhythmically, she picked one berry after another, but her thoughts were on Aaron; and she kept glancing up, wondering what was taking him so long.

Several minutes later, Aaron showed up. His straw hat was tipped way back on his head, and his face was red and sweaty.

"What happened?" she asked as he knelt beside her. "You look like you've been running."

"That stupid horse of mine decided he wanted to trot awhile before I got him locked in the corral. I chased the silly critter around the barn twice before I finally caught up to him."

Since the barn was on the side of the house and the garden was out back, Allison hadn't been able to see the incident, but she imagined it must have looked pretty funny. She held back the laughter bubbling in her throat and pointed to her half-full bucket of berries. "You can help fill mine if you want. When it's full, we can get another container for you to take home."

"Sounds *gut*." Aaron wiped his forehead with his shirtsleeve and started picking.

❧

During the next hour, the two couples cleaned up most of the ripe berries. When they were done, they sat in wicker chairs on the back porch, drinking tall glasses of cold milk and eating the brownies Katie's mamm had made.

As the sun began to set, Allison stood and smoothed the wrinkles in her dark purple dress. "Guess I'd better be going. Uncle Ben and Aunt Mary will worry if I'm out after dark."

Aaron jumped up. "I've got an idea. Why don't I drive you home in your buggy, and Joseph can take our rig?"

"How will you get home once you've dropped me off?" she questioned.

Aaron rubbed the bridge of his nose as he contemplated the problem.

"I know how we can make it work," Joseph spoke up. "I'll stay and visit with Katie awhile, and that'll give you a chance to take Allison home. When I'm ready to head out, I'll swing by the Kings' place and pick you up."

"That's fine by me." Aaron glanced at Allison. "Are you okay with it?"

She nodded. "*Allerdings*—sure enough."

❧

The breeze hitting Allison's face as they traveled in the buggy helped her cool off, but when Aaron guided the horse to a wide spot alongside the road and slipped his arm across her shoulders, her face heated up.

He grinned at her. "Hope ya don't mind that I stopped, but it's hard to talk with the wind in our faces and the horse snortin' the way he does. It's not very romantic either."

Allison smiled. "No, I don't mind your stopping."

"I really enjoy bein' with you," Aaron said, leaning closer. He smelled good, like ripe strawberries and fresh wind.

She opened her mouth to reply, but his lips touched hers before she could get a word out. The kiss was gentle yet firm, and Allison slipped her hands around Aaron's neck as she leaned into him, enjoying the pleasant moment they shared.

The *clomp-clomp* of horse's hooves, followed by a horn honking, broke the spell, and she reluctantly pulled away. "I—I think a buggy and a car must be coming."

Aaron nodded and reached for her hand. "Just sit tight and let 'em pass."

As the two vehicles drew closer, Allison's mouth dropped open. The horse was trotting fast in one lane, and the car, going the same way, sped along in the other lane.

"That car is attempting to pass, but the *mopskopp*—stupid fellow—in the buggy is tryin' to race him," Aaron said with a shake of his head.

Allison sat there, too stunned to say a word. She could hardly believe the buggy driver would try to keep up with a car.

"That's James Esh in his fancy rig," Aaron mumbled. "He hasn't got a lick of sense."

The buggy raced past them so quickly, Allison felt a chilly breeze. Suddenly, the horse whinnied, reared up, and swerved into the side of the car.

twenty-one

Allison gasped as she watched James's buggy careen into the car, bounce away, swerve back and forth, and finally flip over on its side. The panicked horse broke free and tore off down the road, and James flew out of the buggy, landing in the ditch with a terrible thud.

The car screeched to a stop, the Englisher jumped out, and Allison and Aaron hopped down from the buggy. "I didn't hit that fellow on purpose," the middle-aged man said in a trembling voice. "He was trying to keep me from passing and kept swerving all over the road." He raked a shaking hand through his thinning brown hair and winced as his gaze came to rest on James, who lay motionless in a twisted position.

From where Allison stood, she couldn't see the extent of James's injuries, and as the man and Aaron rushed over to him, she could only stand there, too dazed to move. She saw the English man bend down and touch the side of James's neck; then he reached into his shirt pocket and pulled out a cell phone. Aaron's lips moved, but she wasn't able to make out his words.

Allison's heart pounded wildly as a vision from the past threatened to suffocate her. Taking short, quick breaths, she leaned against her buggy. . . .

Mama. She saw her mamm's buggy leaving their driveway and pulling onto the road. She heard the sound of screeching brakes, a horse's high-pitched whinny, and her mother's shrill scream.

Allison squeezed her eyes shut, and the image became clearer. The car slammed into Mama's buggy, thrusting it to the middle of the street before it toppled on its side with a sickening clatter.

"Mama! Mama!" Allison had rushed into the road, but someone—maybe the English man who'd driven the car, pushed her aside.

Allison struggled to bring her thoughts back to the present and had to lean over and place both hands on her knees in order to get her heartbeat to slow. "I remember," she murmured. "I remember seeing Mama's accident on that hot summer day."

She glanced over at James again and noticed that the lower part of his body had been covered with a quilt. Aaron must have taken it from the back of her buggy without her realizing it.

When Aaron and the English man joined Allison again, she noticed that Aaron stood in such a way that her view of James was blocked. She wondered if he was trying to shield her from seeing the extent of James's injuries.

"Is—is James dead?" Allison's voice was little more than a gravelly croak, and the moisture on her cheeks dribbled all the way to her chin.

"There's a faint pulse, but it doesn't look good," the English man answered before Aaron could reply. "I've called 9-1-1 on my cell phone, and an ambulance is on its way."

"I—I need to see James. There's something I must tell him." Allison stepped around Aaron, but he grabbed hold of her arm.

"He's not conscious, and there's nothing we can do but wait for help to arrive."

"Shouldn't we get him up off the ground?"

"That's not a good idea," the English man said. "He's likely got internal injuries, and from the looks of his left leg, I'd say he has at least one broken bone."

Allison swallowed around the lump in her throat. "I have to talk to James."

Aaron shook his head. "You don't want to go over there, believe me. He's been seriously injured, and—"

"And it's not a pretty sight," the Englisher interrupted. "You'd better listen to your boyfriend and wait in the buggy."

"No, I won't!" Allison pulled away from Aaron's grasp.

"Then let me go with you," he offered.

"I'd rather do this alone." Without waiting for Aaron's reply, she rushed over to James and knelt beside his mangled body. Her heart lurched at the sight of his head, twisted awkwardly to one side and covered in blood. His left leg was bent at an odd, distorted angle, and his arms were both scraped and bleeding.

"James. Can you hear me?"

There was no response—no indication that he was even alive.

Heavenly Father, Allison prayed, *help me get through to him. Please don't let it be too late for James.*

With her eyes closed, Allison quoted the verse of Scripture from Jeremiah 29:13 that Aunt Mary had shared with her. " 'And ye shall seek me, and find me, when ye shall search for me with all your heart.' "

Allison heard a muffled moan, and her eyes popped open. James's eyes were open, and even though they were mere slits, she was confident that he could see her.

"James, have you ever asked God to forgive your sins? Have you accepted Jesus as your personal Savior?" she whispered, leaning close to his ear.

His only response was another weak moan.

She laid a gentle hand on James's chest. It was the only place on his body where there was no blood showing. "If you can hear me, blink your eyes once."

His eyelids closed then opened slowly again.

"I'm going to pray with you, James. If you believe the words I say, then repeat them in your mind."

James closed his eyes, but the slight rise and fall of his chest let Allison know he was still breathing.

"Dear Lord," she prayed, "I know I'm a sinner, and I ask Your forgiveness for the wrongs I have done. I believe Jesus died on the cross for my sins, and that His blood saves me now."

When Allison finished the prayer, James opened his eyes and blinked once. Had she gotten through to him? Had he sought the Lord's forgiveness and yielded his life to Him?

Sirens blared in the distance, and Allison felt a sense of

peace. She'd done all she could for the man who lay before her. James's life was in God's hands.

❧

As Aaron watched Allison kneeling beside James's wounded body, a pang of jealousy crept into his soul. Only moments ago, she and Aaron had been kissing. Now she was at James's side, whispering in his ear.

I feel bad for the poor fellow and hate being a witness to such a terrible accident. Even though I've never cared much for James Esh, I find no pleasure in him getting hurt or possibly dying. Aaron grimaced. He hoped James's injuries weren't life threatening and had even said a prayer on his behalf. Yet Aaron couldn't set his feelings of rejection aside as he witnessed Allison with a man she supposedly cared nothing about. She obviously had stronger feelings for James than she'd been willing to admit.

Aaron gritted his teeth. *If it were me layin' there hurt, would she care so much?* He was tempted to move closer so he could hear what she was saying, but that might make things worse. If Allison did love James, she might see Aaron's coming over as interference. She needed this time to express her feelings and possibly say her last good-byes. No, Aaron would not disturb their time together, no matter how much he wanted to know what was being said.

A blaring siren drove his thoughts aside, and he felt relief when the ambulance and a police car approached the scene of the accident. Two paramedics rushed over to James, while a policeman headed for the English man, waiting beside his car.

Aaron stepped forward, knowing that he was a witness to the crash and should tell the police everything he'd seen.

Just before Aaron approached the uniformed officer, he glanced over his shoulder. The paramedics had lifted James onto a stretcher, and Allison followed as they headed for the ambulance. Was she planning to go with them to the hospital?

Aaron squeezed his eyes shut. *Lord, please be with James, and give me the strength to let Allison go, for it appears we're not meant to be together.*

twenty-two

Allison drew in a deep breath and tried to steady her nerves. Today was the Saturday the men in the community had planned to build Uncle Ben's new barn. Instead, they stood at the cemetery, saying good-bye to James Esh. The barn raising would have to wait another week or so.

While Allison felt sure James had heard the prayer she'd offered on his behalf and found forgiveness for his sins, she grieved for his family. It didn't seem right that a young man in the prime of his life had been killed in such a senseless, tragic accident.

She pitied Clarence and Alma Esh, whose only son hadn't been baptized so he could become a member of the church before his untimely death. Allison knew that some in this community believed James's soul had been lost because he'd acted so crazily and not joined the church. She hoped for the chance to speak with his parents later on and explain how she had been able to pray with their son before he died. It might offer some measure of comfort if they knew James had been given the opportunity to make things right with God.

Allison glanced at her friend Katie, who stood with her folks next to James's family. Katie's eyes were downcast, as were the rest of the family's, and Alma Esh leaned her head on her husband's shoulder as she trembled with obvious grief.

Allison felt moisture on her cheek and realized that she, too, was crying. She knew it was partly in sympathy for James's family, but she also grieved for her mother's passing. It had been hard to witness James's tragic accident, and remembering the crash that had taken her mamm's life was nearly Allison's undoing. Even now, as she tried to focus on the verses of scripture Bishop Frey quoted, she could picture Mama lying in the street after being tossed from her buggy when the car had smashed into her. There'd been no chance for good-byes, no opportunity to touch her dear mamm one last time. Allison's brothers, Ezra and Gerald, had insisted she and Peter go up to the house while Papa waited with Mama until the ambulance arrived. Peter went willingly, but Allison remembered sobbing and begging to stay. Ezra had threatened to carry her if she didn't cooperate, so Allison had remained in the house all afternoon, waiting for some word on her mother's condition. Papa and her oldest brothers, Cleon and Milton, didn't return from the hospital until that evening with the grim news that Mama had passed away. That's when Allison fell apart and her memory of the accident shut down.

With a determination to leave the past behind, Allison's gaze went to Aaron, who stood between Joseph and Zachary. Aaron's parents, his youngest brother, and two sisters stood behind the three oldest brothers, and each wore a somber expression.

Allison hoped Aaron would look her way so she could offer a smile or nod of encouragement, but the one time he did glance in her direction, he frowned and looked quickly away.

Aaron had seemed distant toward her since the evening of James's accident, and Allison didn't know why. She thought about the way she hadn't been allowed to accompany James to the hospital, since she wasn't a family member. Also, the police wanted to ask her about the things she had witnessed. So Allison, Aaron, and the English man who'd driven the vehicle that collided with James's buggy sat in the police car answering questions, while James was rushed to Springfield. It wasn't until the following morning that Allison learned James had died en route to the hospital.

Allison hadn't realized at first that Aaron was acting differently toward her. He'd said only a few words and seemed almost as if he were in daze when she'd joined him in the police car for questioning. She'd thought he was upset over witnessing the horrible crash. But then Joseph showed up, and Aaron suggested his brother take Allison home while he drove over to James's house to tell his parents what had happened. Later, when Aaron came back to Uncle Ben and Aunt Mary's to pick up Joseph, Allison had hoped they could talk. However, Aaron said he and his brother needed to get home, and they'd left in a hurry. Aaron never came around the rest of the week.

Allison squeezed her eyes shut. *What's gone wrong between Aaron and me?* A silent prayer floated through her mind. *Oh, Lord, please give me the opportunity to speak with Aaron today. And if it's Your will for us to be a couple, then make things right between us again.*

Another thought popped into Allison's mind. Maybe Aaron wasn't upset with her at all. He might be grieving over James's death or feeling guilty for the unkind words he'd said about James when he was alive. Not that those things weren't true. Allison had seen for herself how irritating James could be, and she'd never doubted anything Aaron had said. Still, she knew it wasn't right to talk about someone behind his back, and if Aaron felt guilty, that might be the reason for his distant attitude. She prayed that was all there was to it, and she hoped she'd have a chance to speak with Aaron after the funeral dinner. If there was any possibility of them having a permanent relationship, they needed to clear the air.

❧

Aaron tried to concentrate on the eulogy Bishop Frey was giving as the man stood at the head of James's casket. But it was hard not to think about Allison and how their relationship had crumbled on the night of James's death. Aaron had thought they were drawing close, and that she might even be falling in love with him. But when he'd seen her reaction to the accident, heard the panic in her voice when she insisted on seeing James, and watched her bend over James's body as though she was his girlfriend, he'd been hit with the realization that Allison loved James, not him.

Aaron clenched his fingers as he held his hands rigidly at his sides. *That's what I get for allowing myself to fall in love. It was stupid to think Allison might become my wife someday. Now I wish I'd never gone anywhere with her.* He swallowed around the nodule in his throat as a sense of despair crept into his soul, pushing cracks of doubt that threatened his confidence and smashed the notion that he'd finally found the perfect woman for him. *From now on, I'm going to concentrate on my work and forget about Allison loving me, for it's obviously not meant to be.*

Aaron turned his thoughts to the harness shop. He'd had a disagreement with his stepfather yesterday morning. Paul had said Aaron was careless and sometimes seemed lazy. Aaron had become angry and reminded Paul that he wasn't his daed and didn't have the right to tell him what to do.

I shouldn't have lost my temper, Aaron berated himself. *Paul's a good man, and I know he loves my mamm. I'm sure he cares about everyone in the family—including me. I should have apologized right away, and I'll do that as soon as we get home.*

Aaron pulled his thoughts aside and concentrated on the bishop's final prayer. It wasn't right that he'd let his mind wander during the graveside service. No matter how much of a scoundrel James Esh had been, he'd passed from this world into the next and deserved everyone's respect during the last phase of his funeral.

⌘

Allison kept busy during the funeral dinner, which was held at Clarence and Alma Esh's house. She helped the women serve the meal and clean up afterward, and was pleased to see that all of the strawberry pies she and Aunt Mary had made had been eaten. By the time the last dish was put away, some people had already headed for home. Allison hoped Aaron and his family were not among them. She hadn't seen Barbara or Paul Hilty since they'd eaten, so she knew they were either outside or had already gone home. Of course, even if they had left, it didn't mean Aaron or his brothers had.

Allison stepped onto the front porch and scanned the yard. Some of the older men sat in chairs under a leafy maple tree, a group of children played nearby, and several women had gathered in another area. No sign of Aaron or anyone from his family, though. *Maybe he's in the barn.* She headed that way, kicking up dust with each step she took. It had been a dry summer, and they were in need of some rain.

Inside the barn, Allison spotted Joseph and Katie sitting on a bale of straw next to Gabe and Melinda. She hurried over and tapped Joseph on the shoulder. "Is Aaron still here? I need to speak with him."

Joseph shook his head. "Sorry, but he left when our folks did. Grandpa and Grandma Raber were tired and needed to get home. I guess Aaron didn't feel like hanging around because he followed them in his buggy. Emma, Bessie, and Davey rode with him, too. Zachary and I are the only ones from our family still here."

Allison felt a keen sense of disappointment. She would have to speak with Aaron some other time. "I plan to take some of my faceless dolls to the gift shop at the bed-and-breakfast in Seymour on Monday morning," she said. "Maybe I'll drop by the harness shop on my way to town."

"I'm sure Aaron will be glad to see you," Joseph replied.

Allison's only reply was a quick nod. She wasn't convinced that he would be pleased to see her. In fact, if Aaron was miffed for some reason, he might even ask her to leave. She was prepared to exit the barn when Katie said, "Won't you sit and visit awhile?"

"I'd better not. Aunt Mary and the rest of the family will be ready to leave soon, and I don't want to keep them waiting."

"Gabe and I would like to get together with you and Aaron soon and go fishing again." Melinda rubbed her protruding stomach and glanced over at Katie. "Maybe you and Joseph can join us."

Katie and Joseph nodded, but Allison merely shrugged and said, "I'll have to wait and see. Right now I need to speak with Clarence and Alma Esh." She turned and rushed from the barn.

twenty-three

Allison waved good-bye to Aunt Mary, clucked to the horse, and guided her buggy down the driveway. She was excited about taking some of her dolls to the bed-and-breakfast in town but felt nervous about stopping at the harness shop to speak with Aaron. Would he be glad to see her? Would he be too busy to talk? Could they get their relationship back to where it had been before James's accident?

She whispered a prayer. "Heavenly Father, please give me the right words to say to Aaron, and help him be willing to talk things through."

Allison thought of a verse of scripture she'd read in Proverbs 18:24 that morning. *"A man that hath friends must shew himself friendly: and there is a friend that sticketh closer than a brother."* She wanted to be Aaron's friend, even if she couldn't be his *aldi*—girlfriend. She knew if he was grieving over James's death, he needed her as a friend. And if he wanted more than a simple friendship, he might be glad when she told him what her daed said in the letter she had received that morning.

As her horse and buggy proceeded down Highway C, Allison tried to focus on other things. It was a warm morning, already muggy and buzzing with insects. She'd been swatting at flies ever since she left her aunt and uncle's place.

Allison wondered what it would be like to spend a winter in Webster County. Since the Amish who lived here only drove open buggies, she knew she would have to bundle up in order to be protected when the weather turned cold and snowy. Even so, she longed to stay in this small Amish community, where she could be close to the family and friends she had come to care about.

Her thoughts went to James and how disappointed his

parents were that he hadn't joined the church. When she'd sought them out after the funeral dinner, they'd told her how they had hoped James would settle down and marry a nice Amish woman from their community and said it was hard to accept his death. Alma Esh confided that she feared her son had not made it to heaven. But when Allison told them about the prayer she'd said with James, both of his parents seemed comforted.

Bringing her thoughts back to the present, Allison guided the horse to turn at the entrance of the Hiltys' place. She halted him in front of the hitching post by the harness shop and stepped down from the buggy. It was time to see Aaron.

❧

"I'm going up to the house to speak with your mamm, but I'll be back soon," Paul called to Aaron, who knelt on the floor in front of a metal tub filled with dark dye. "Is there anything I can bring you to eat or drink?"

Aaron looked up from his job and smiled. He was glad he had apologized to his stepfather for the harsh words he'd spoken the other morning. Paul had asked Aaron's forgiveness, too, and things seemed better between them now. "How about a couple of Mom's oatmeal cookies?"

"Sure, I can do that." Paul opened the door and had no more than stepped outside when Allison walked in.

"Gude mariye, Paul," she said. "I'm on my way to Seymour and thought I'd drop by and see Aaron a few minutes. If he's not too busy, that is."

Paul nodded. "I'm heading up to the house, and Aaron's dying some leather straps, but you're welcome to come inside and talk to him."

As Allison moved toward Aaron, his breath caught in his throat. He waited for Paul to shut the door then held up his hands, which were encased in rubber gloves and dark with stain. "Better not get too close. This stuff is hard to scrub off if you get any on your clothes or skin."

"I'll be careful."

"What did you want to see me about?" he asked, moistening his lips, which felt awfully dry.

Allison leaned against the nearby workbench. "We haven't had the chance to talk since the night of James's accident. I'd wanted to speak with you after the funeral dinner, but Joseph said you had gone home with your folks."

Aaron's only reply was a quick nod.

She cleared her throat. "You've been acting kind of distant, and I'm wondering if there's something wrong."

Aaron draped the piece of leather he'd stained over a rung on the wooden drying rack and stood. Should he tell her what he thought about her reaction to James? Would it do any good to share his feelings?

"Are you upset about James?" Allison questioned.

He nodded. Maybe she had figured things out already.

"If you're feeling guilty because you said unkind things about James before he died, all you need to do is confess it to God."

Aaron's mouth dropped open. "What?"

"You seemed so glum during the funeral service, and I wondered if it was because you felt remorseful and wished you could have made things right between you and James before he died."

"I do feel bad for speakin' out against him, even though the things I said were true," Aaron admitted.

"It's easy to let things slip off our tongue when we're upset. I should know; I've done plenty of it in the past—especially before I had a personal relationship with God." Allison took a step toward Aaron, but he held up his hands.

"Stain, remember?"

"Right." She smiled. "So the reason you didn't say much when you took me home after the accident was because you felt bad about the way things had been between you and James?"

"Actually, I wasn't talking much because I was upset over *you* and James."

"Me and James?"

"Jah. The way you acted when he was thrown from his buggy made me think you had strong feelings for him."

Allison's mouth hung wide open. "You really thought that?"

He nodded. "You were determined to speak with James, and then you wanted to ride to the hospital in the ambulance with him. It made me believe—"

"I did care about James, but not in the way you might think," she interrupted.

"How was it then?"

"I cared about his soul—and where he would spend eternity if he died."

Aaron shifted from one foot to the other. Was Allison saying she had rushed to James's side in order to speak to him about God?

"I told James he could be forgiven of his sins, and then I prayed, asking him to repeat the prayer in his mind." Allison smiled, even though there were tears in her eyes. "I think James understood, and I believe he's in heaven right now."

Aaron felt as if someone had squeezed all the air out of his lungs. If Allison wasn't in love with James, was it possible that she cared for him?

She stepped forward and touched his arm. "Are you okay? Have I said something to upset you?"

He pulled the rubber gloves off his hands and let them fall to the floor, then quickly reached for her hand. "I've been so dumm."

"Why would you say that, Aaron?"

"I'm dumb for thinkin' you loved James, and dumber yet for thinkin' you'd led me to believe you might care for me." He hung his head, unable to meet her gaze. "It's taken me a long time to deal with my feelings about my daed's death and how it affected my mamm afterward. I was scared of falling in love and gettin' married because I was worried that my wife might be taken away." He drew in a deep breath and looked into her eyes. "After talking to Mom several weeks ago, I finally realized that God gave her a second chance at love with Paul and that we can't live our lives in fear of the unknown."

"That's true."

"I have always told everyone that I'd never get married because I couldn't find the kind of woman I needed. But then you came along, and that all changed."

Allison's forehead wrinkled. "How can you think I'm the kind of woman you need? I can barely cook, and the things I enjoy doing most are considered men's jobs."

He grinned and lifted her chin with his thumb. "That's what I like about you—you're not afraid to try some things other women might shy away from." He wiggled his eyebrows. "I'm sure in time you'll learn to cook well, too."

Allison smiled. "I got a letter from my daed this morning, giving me permission to stay here longer."

"That's gut news!" Aaron drew her into his arms, not even caring that Paul might step through the door at any moment. "I thank the Lord you came by today," he murmured in her ear.

twenty-four

Two weeks later, on a Saturday morning, Allison awoke with a feeling of anticipation. Today was the day of Uncle Ben's barn raising, and Aaron would be here, along with most of the Amish men in their community. It would be a long day, and she knew the men would be arriving soon, so she needed to hurry and get downstairs to help Aunt Mary and Sarah in the kitchen. She also knew several women would be coming with their husbands, so they would have plenty of help throughout the day.

Allison headed down the stairs and met her aunt in the hallway. "Gude mariye," Aunt Mary said. "Did you sleep well?"

"Jah. And you?"

"I slept fine, except I'm wishin' I had gone to bed earlier last night. I'll need a lot of energy to get through the day."

"I'll help wherever I'm needed."

"I know you will." Aunt Mary squeezed Allison's arm. "You've been a big help since you came here, and I'm glad you'll be staying longer."

Allison smiled. "Me, too."

"Oh, I almost forgot—when I was in Seymour at the chiropractor's yesterday, I was telling the doctor's receptionist about your faceless dolls. She has a friend who works at a gift shop in Branson, and she'd like to sell some of your dolls in her shop."

"That would be wunderbaar," Allison said excitedly. "I've got several made up, so maybe I could run them by the chiropractor's office on Monday morning."

"I might go with you," Aunt Mary said as they entered the kitchen. "Then I can see if the doctor has time to work on my back again. After today, I'll probably need another adjustment."

"If you're hurting, why don't you rest and let me take over? I'm sure there will be plenty of other women here to help, too."

Aunt Mary shook her head. "I wouldn't dream of putting all the responsibility on your shoulders. I'll be fine as long as I don't lift anything heavy."

"We'll just have to see that you don't." Allison gave her aunt a quick hug, grabbed her choring apron from the wall peg by the back door, and hurried to the refrigerator. There was so much to be thankful for, and she was eager to begin the day.

❧

"How come you two are wearin' such big grins on your faces? Are ya anxious to spend the day workin' up a sweat?" Zachary sat on the front seat between Aaron and Joseph as they rode in Aaron's buggy, heading for the Kings' place. He gave them each a nudge with his bony elbows. "I'll bet I know why you've got such smug expressions. Your girlfriends will be there today, and you can't wait to see 'em."

"Knock it off, or we'll put you in the backseat," Aaron warned.

"Ha!" Zachary's forehead wrinkled. "Maybe I should have ridden with Pop and Davey."

"That might have been for the best," Joseph said, nudging Zachary's shoulder. "At least they'd be the ones puttin' up with you now, and Aaron and I would be ridin' in peace and quiet."

The rest of the trip went pretty much the same, with Zachary trying to get Joseph and Aaron to admit that the reason they were in good spirits was because they were both in *lieb*.

Zachary's right; I am in love, Aaron thought as he snapped the reins to get the horse moving faster. *But I'm not about to admit that to my little brother. It would be just like him to blab, and then I'd have to take all kinds of ribbing, especially from Gabe.*

Aaron thought about his best friend and how he would soon become a father. There was a time when the idea of having kinner scared Aaron to death. Not anymore, though. Now that he and Allison had worked things out, and she'd gotten news that she could stay longer, he was hopeful they might have a future together. If they ever did decide to get married, he hoped Allison would be willing to live in Missouri. He had no desire to move, especially not to Pennsylvania, where there were so many tourists.

"I'm glad we're finally here," Joseph said as they pulled onto the Kings' property. "You want me and Zachary to help you with the horse, or should the two of us start helpin' on the barn?"

"I can manage on my own," Aaron replied. "I'll join you as soon as I get the horse situated in the corral."

"Okay." Joseph jumped down, and Zachary did the same. As soon as they'd moved away, Aaron drove his rig to the area where several other buggies were parked. He'd just gotten the horse unhitched when his best friend showed up.

"You all set for a good day's work?" Gabe asked with a smile.

"Sure. How about you?"

Gabe nodded. "I'm happy whenever I'm building anything."

"I'll bet you are."

"I can probably get started on Rufus's dog run some evening next week. Would that work for you?"

"Jah. Whenever you have the time."

"You look a lot happier today than the last I saw you," Gabe commented. "Is there anything going on that I should know about?"

Aaron snickered. "Is there anything you don't already know?"

Gabe slapped him playfully on the back. "Are you sayin' I'm nosy?"

"I'm not saying that at all. You just seem to have a way of knowin' what's goin' on around our community."

"Guess that's because so many of my customers like to share the local news." Gabe wiggled his eyebrows and chuckled.

"Jah, well, you need to be careful you don't blab all that ya hear. Some folks don't like others knowin' their business."

"Like you? Is that what you're sayin'?"

Aaron merely shrugged and led his horse into the corral. He knew Gabe was only funning with him, but he'd put up with enough ribbing on the ride over here.

"So you're not gonna tell me what's put such a silly grin on your face this morning?"

Aaron closed the corral gate and turned to face his friend. "If you must know, Allison got a letter from her daed the other day, and she'll be stickin' around here longer than the end of summer."

"Oh? How long is she plannin' to stay?"

"Don't rightly know. Guess that all depends on how things go."

"You mean between you and her?"

Aaron nodded. "Allison and I are going to start courtin' on a regular basis."

Gabe's face broke into a wide smile, and he thumped Aaron on the back. "That's gut news! By this time next year, you could be an old married man."

Aaron laughed. "Married, maybe, but not old." He glanced around, hoping to catch a glimpse of Allison, but she was nowhere in sight. *Probably inside with the women fixing snacks and gettin' the noon meal going. Maybe we can spend a few minutes together after lunch. If not, I'll make a point to speak to her before I head home.*

Gabe motioned to the group of men already wielding hammers and saws. "Well, I suppose we've gabbed long enough. It's time to get busy."

"Jah," Aaron agreed. "Let's *mach dich an die arewet*—get to work!"

◈

"Why don't you and I serve that table over there?" Allison suggested to Katie as she motioned to the wooden plank set on two sawhorses where Aaron and Joseph sat with several other young men.

"That's fine with me," Katie replied with a twinkle in her eyes.

Allison grabbed a platter of sandwiches from the serving table, and Katie reached for a jug of cold lemonade.

When Allison set the plate in front of Aaron, he smiled and whispered, "It's gut to see you. Have ya been workin' hard all mornin'?"

She nodded. "Not nearly as hard as you, though. It's awful hot today. Have you been getting enough to drink?"

"Jah. Sarah and Bessie have brought water to the crew several times this morning."

"Hey, are you gonna pass those sandwiches over, or did ya plan to spend your lunch hour gabbin'?" Zachary, who sat across from Aaron, held out his hand. "I'm starvin' here."

Aaron grabbed a ham sandwich, plunked it on his paper plate, and handed it to the next man in line. "Maybe there won't be any sandwiches left by the time they get around to you, little brother," he teased.

"Don't pay him any mind, Zachary," Allison put in. "There's plenty more sandwiches in the kitchen." She enjoyed this bantering with Aaron and his younger brother. It reminded her of the times she and Peter had teased each other.

"Aw, you're no fun." Aaron winked at her. "Just kidding."

Allison smiled and moved back to the serving table to get a bag of potato chips. When she returned, she was surprised to see that Aaron wasn't in his seat. Surely he couldn't have finished eating already. He hadn't even had dessert.

"Allison—over here."

She turned around. Aaron was crouched in the flower bed near the back porch. "What are you doing down there?"

"I spotted this and wondered if it was yours." He held a tiny white kapp between his thumb and index finger.

Allison squinted. It looked like one of the head coverings she'd made for her faceless dolls. But how would it have gotten out here? "Let me have a look at that." She took the tiny hat from Aaron and studied the stitching. It had been done by hand, not on the treadle machine, and she knew immediately whose it was. "This isn't one I made. It belongs on the little doll my mamm sewed for me before she died." She shook her head. "I don't understand how it got out of my room and ended up in the flower bed. I've never taken that doll off the foot of my bed."

Aaron stood. "Maybe one of the kinner who came with their folks today wandered into your room and discovered the doll."

"I guess I should go inside and take a look." She tucked the kapp in the pocket of her apron and started to turn around.

"Uh. . .before you go, I was wondering if we could plan another day of fishing soon. Maybe we could invite an old married couple along as chaperones."

"You mean Gabe and Melinda?"

"Jah. We had fun with them the last time, don't ya think?"

She nodded. "Sounds fine to me. When did you want to go?"

"Well, I was thinkin' maybe—"

"Hey, Allison, the mail just came, and there's a letter for you," her cousin Dan interrupted. He held the envelope out to her and grinned.

I wonder if that little stinker intruded on purpose. Allison took the letter. "Danki, Dan."

He stood there, as though waiting for something. "Well, aren't ya gonna open it? It could be important, ya know."

Allison glanced at the envelope in her hand. One look at the return address and she knew it was from her daed. "That's strange," she murmured. "I just got a letter from Papa a few weeks ago. It's not like him to write again so soon. Maybe it's something important." She took a seat on the porch steps and ripped open the letter.

"Well, guess I'd better get back to the table before all the food's gone," Aaron said.

"Oh, okay. I'll talk to you later then."

Aaron smiled and walked away.

Allison glanced at her young cousin. "Shouldn't you be eating your lunch, too?"

"I'm done."

"Then haven't you got something else to do?"

Dan shrugged his shoulders. "If I go back to the table, Papa will see me. Then he'll expect me to haul more nails and stuff to the men." He wrinkled his nose. "Why can't they see that I'm capable of doin' some real work?"

Anxious to read her daed's letter, Allison decided the only way she was going to have any privacy was to go upstairs. "I've got to run up to my room a minute, Dan. Why don't you ask Aaron or Joseph if there's something you can do to help them this afternoon?"

Dan's mouth curved into a smile. "That's a gut idea. I think Aaron likes me, so he might let me help him pound nails." He turned and darted away.

A few minutes later, Allison sat on the edge of her bed. She pulled Papa's letter from the envelope and read it silently.

Dear Allison,

I think I've mentioned that your aunt Catherine has been having pains in her stomach for some time. I finally talked her into going to the doctor, and just this morning she got the results of the tests that were done. There's no easy way to say this, but my sister has cancer, and the doctor's afraid it's already traveled throughout much of her body.

Allison gasped. Aunt Catherine sick with cancer? No, it couldn't be. She sat there several seconds, trying to digest what she had read. Needing to know more, she finished reading the letter.

I know I said you could stay in Webster County as long as you wanted, but we really need you here. Aunt Catherine will be going through more tests and might undergo chemo or radiation. She won't have the energy to cook, clean, or care for the house, so I'm asking you to come home as soon as possible.

Love,
Papa

Allison let the letter slip from her fingers as tears clouded her vision. "Oh, dear God, please don't let Aunt Catherine die before I get home. I need the chance to speak with her."

twenty-five

As Allison stood with Aunt Mary in front of Lazy Lee's Gas Station on Monday morning, tears welled up in her eyes and mixed with the raindrops that had begun to fall. The much-needed rain they'd all been praying for was finally here, and it seemed fitting that the clouds overhead would be adding their tears to her own. Instead of taking her homemade Amish dolls to the chiropractor's office so the receptionist could offer them to a gift shop in Branson, she now waited for a bus that would take her home.

It pained Allison to leave Aunt Mary and her family, and it especially hurt to be going away from Aaron. It had been hard to tell him she was returning to Pennsylvania, and even more difficult to admit that she didn't know when or if she might return to Missouri. She and Aaron had both promised to write, but she knew it wouldn't be easy to carry on a long-distance relationship. She wished she could have offered Aaron a guarantee that she would come back, but there were no guarantees. She didn't know how long she would be needed at home, and if Aunt Catherine should die, Papa would need someone to cook and keep house for him.

Last night, after a light supper at her aunt and uncle's place, Allison and Aaron had gone for a buggy ride. They'd decided that was the best way to say their good-byes. She could still see the forlorn look on Aaron's face after he kissed her one final time. In her heart, she longed to say she loved him and ask if he would wait for her. But that wouldn't have been fair. As much as it hurt to acknowledge that she might have to stay in Pennsylvania indefinitely, Allison knew if that happened, she would have to let Aaron go. He deserved the freedom to move on with his life and find someone else to marry.

"We'll surely miss you," Aunt Mary said, breaking into Allison's thoughts. "And we will pray that God might offer a miracle for your daed's sister."

Allison nodded. "It would be wunderbaar if she was healed of her cancer, but I'm more worried about her soul."

"We'll be praying about that, too." Aunt Mary smiled and slipped her arm around Allison's waist. "I will ask God to give you the chance to witness to her, just as you did with James."

"Danki." Allison glanced over her shoulder. A part of her had secretly hoped Aaron would come to see her off this morning. But maybe it was for the best that he hadn't shown up. A tearful good-bye in front of Aunt Mary or anyone else waiting for the bus would have been too difficult. It was better that she and Aaron had given their good-byes to each other last night.

"I appreciate your willingness to try to sell the dolls I'm leaving with you," Allison said, hoping the change of subject might lessen her pain. "There wouldn't be much point in me taking them with me."

"I don't mind a'tall," Aunt Mary replied. "But I do hope you will continue making faceless dolls when you get home."

Allison shook her head. "I doubt there'll be time for that, since I'll have so many chores to do. Not to mention that I'll be needed to help care for Aunt Catherine as she goes through her cancer treatments."

"I understand, but if you do find any free time, sewing might be good therapy for you."

"I'll have to see how it goes." Allison looked at the piece of luggage sitting at her feet. All the clothes she had brought to Missouri were inside the suitcase, but one important item was missing—the little faceless doll Mama had made for her before she died. It didn't feel right leaving without that precious doll; yet all that remained of it was the small white kapp Aaron had found in the flower bed. When Allison had gone to her room on Saturday to read the letter from Papa, she had discovered the doll was not on her bed. After a thorough search of the room, she'd resigned herself to the fact that someone must have taken it, probably that same day. She had questioned several people and searched the house and barn, but the doll hadn't turned up anywhere.

"If you should ever find the faceless doll my mamm made, would you mail it to me?" Allison asked Aunt Mary.

"Of course, and I'll ask everyone in the family to keep looking for it, too."

The rumble of the Greyhound bus pulling into the parking lot brought a fresh set of tears to Allison's eyes. She was about to leave Webster County behind, along with so many people she had come to love. *At least I'm returning home a little better equipped to run a house, and for that I feel thankful.*

While her suitcase was being loaded into the baggage compartment, Allison turned and gave Aunt Mary a hug. "Danki for everything—especially for showing me how to find the Lord." Her voice broke and she swallowed hard. "Come visit us sometime if you can."

Aunt Mary nodded as tears ran down her cheeks. "I'll be praying that you'll be able to come back here again, too."

❧

As Aaron guided his horse and buggy into Lazy Lee's, he scanned the parking lot, filled with numerous mud puddles. There was no sign of Allison or her aunt out front. Had he arrived too late to give her one final kiss good-bye?

A vision of Allison's sweet face popped into his head. He could still see her sad expression as they stood on the Kings' front porch last night after their buggy ride. He could feel her soft lips against his own, smell the aroma of peaches from her freshly shampooed hair, and hear the pain in her voice as she murmured, "I'll write as often as I can."

Aaron pulled on the reins and halted his horse near the back of the station, where a hitching rail had been erected for Amish buggies. Maybe the bus hadn't come yet. Allison might be waiting inside, out of the rain. He jumped down from the buggy, tied the horse to the rail, and dashed into the building.

Aaron glanced around the place, noting the numerous racks of fast-food items and shelves full of oil cans, wiper blades, and other things the Englishers used on their cars. A man and a woman sat at one of the tables near the front of the store, eating sub sandwiches, which were sold on the other side of the building. But there was no sign of Allison Troyer or Mary King. Could they have gone to the ladies' room?

"Has the Greyhound bus come in yet?" Aaron asked the middle-aged man behind the counter.

"Yep. Came and left again."

"How long ago?" It was a crazy notion, but if the bus wasn't too far ahead, maybe he could catch up to it along the highway.

"It's been a good ten or fifteen minutes now," the station attendant replied.

Aaron's heart took a nosedive. He was too late. There was no hope of him catching the bus now; it was well on its way to Springfield. He'd thought saying good-bye to Allison last night would be good enough, but this morning as he was getting ready for work, Aaron had changed his mind. With Paul's permission, he'd hitched one of their horses to his buggy and headed for Seymour, with the need to see Allison burning in his soul. He'd wanted to hold her one last time, and let her know how much he loved her.

"You wantin' to buy anything?"

The question from the store clerk halted Aaron's thoughts. "Uh—no. Just came in to see if the bus had come yet."

"As I said before, you've missed it."

With shoulders slumped and head down, Aaron shuffled to the front door, feeling like a heavy chunk of leather was weighing him down. *Will I ever see Allison again?*

twenty-six

"I want you to be prepared for the way things are at home," Allison's father said, as their English neighbor, Eric Swanson, drove them away from the bus station in his minivan.

Allison turned in her seat and faced her daed. "What do you mean, Papa?" His grave expression let her know things weren't good.

"Aunt Catherine has gone into denial since she was diagnosed with cancer. She won't accept any of the treatments the doctors have suggested, and she won't even talk about her illness." He paused and reached for Allison's hand. "She's irritable and tries to do more than she can. Then she exhausts herself and ends up unable to do anything except rest for the next several days. Peter and I can fend for ourselves when it's necessary, but we don't have time to cook decent meals or keep the place clean. And someone needs to be at the house to take care of my sister whenever she's havin' a bad day."

"Maybe she will rest more with me there to do the cleaning and cooking."

Papa nodded soberly. "That's what I'm hopin', and I thank you for coming."

"You're welcome." Allison leaned her head against the seat as she tried to relax. She knew the days ahead would be full of trials. She could only hope she was up to the task.

❧

"Wie geht's?" Gabe asked as he stepped into the harness shop.

Aaron ran his fingers through the back of his hair. "I'm fair to middlin'. How about you?"

"Can't complain." Gabe moved toward the workbench where Aaron stood. "I came over to start workin' on Rufus's dog run. It's about time I got around to it, wouldn't ya say?"

"I suppose."

"You don't sound too enthused. I figured you'd be feelin' desperate to get your mutt off that chain."

Aaron's only response was a noncommittal shrug.

"You seem really *nunner* today."

"You'd be down, too, if the woman you loved had moved to Pennsylvania," Aaron mumbled. He hated feeling depressed and irritable and was tempted to start chewing his nails again.

Gabe shook his head. "Allison didn't *move* to Pennsylvania, Aaron. She lives there and had to return because her aunt is sick."

"I know that."

"She's only been gone a day. I wouldn't think you'd be missin' her already."

"Jah, well, what would you know about how I'm feeling? You're married to the woman you love, and you know that she'll be waitin' for you when you come home every night." Aaron removed his work apron and hung it on a wall peg. It was past quitting time, and Paul had already gone up to the house. Aaron had figured he would stay and work awhile longer, hoping to keep his hands busy and his mind off the emptiness he'd felt since Allison left. Now that Gabe was here, he figured he might as well quit for the day. Truth be told, he was tired and didn't feel like working longer, anyway.

Gabe rested his hand on Aaron's slumped shoulder. "Don't you remember how things were with Melinda and me during our courtship? There was a time when I didn't know if she was going to remain true to her Amish faith, or if she would choose to go English and become a vet." He shook his head. "Don't think that wasn't stressful. Believe me, I know more of how you're feelin' than you can imagine."

Aaron knew his friend was probably right, but it didn't relieve his anxiety any. It had taken a lot for him to get past his feelings about marriage and courting Allison. Knowing they might never be together hurt worse than a kick in the head by an unruly mule.

"Have you had supper yet?" he asked, feeling the need to change the subject.

"I ate a sandwich on the drive over," Gabe replied. "But feel free to go have your meal. I'll get started on the dog run, and when you're done you can join me. If you don't have nothin' else to do, that is."

"I ain't hungry, so I'll show you where I want the run to be built, and then I'll go inside and tell my mamm I won't be joining them at the table this evening."

Gabe clucked his tongue. "You've gotta eat, Aaron. Pinin' for Allison and starvin' yourself won't solve a thing."

Aaron knew his friend was only showing concern, but it irked him nonetheless. He didn't want anyone's sympathy, and he didn't need to be told what to do.

He opened the front door and stepped out, but a blast of hot, muggy air hit him full in the face. He grimaced. "Sure wish it would cool off and rain again. I'm sick of this summer weather!"

Gabe didn't say anything; he just kept on walking.

Aaron kicked at the stones beneath his feet. *Sure hope I get a letter from Allison soon. I really miss her.*

❧

Allison thought she had prepared herself for this moment, but the sight that greeted her when she and Papa stepped into the house made her stomach clench. Aunt Catherine lay on the couch with a wet washrag on her forehead and a hot water bottle on her stomach. Her skin had a grayish-yellow tinge, her eyes were rimmed with dark circles, and she had lost a lot of weight. This wasn't the same robust woman Allison had seen three months ago. It made her wonder how long Aunt Catherine had been sick and hadn't said anything. She might have been in pain for some time, and that could have been the reason she'd been so crabby.

Allison approached the couch, and her aunt struggled to sit. "That's okay. Don't get up on my account." Allison leaned over and took hold of Aunt Catherine's hand. Aunt Catherine squeezed it in return, but there wasn't much strength in the frail woman's grip.

"You shouldn't have come home." Aunt Catherine's words were clipped, and if it hadn't been for the knowledge that the woman was hurting, Allison would have been offended. "I told your daed not to write that letter, but he insisted on bringin' you back to take care of me."

Allison wasn't sure if her aunt didn't want her here because she didn't like her or if the harsh words were spoken because she felt bad about Allison having to leave Missouri. It didn't matter. Allison was home now, and she had a job to do. Many times in the past she'd let Aunt Catherine's sharp tongue bother her, but with God's help, she would care for her aunt's needs—the physical as well as the spiritual.

❧

Over the next several weeks, Allison established a routine. Up early every morning to fix breakfast so Papa and Peter could get out to the milking barn. Clean up the kitchen. Take a tray of hot cereal up to Aunt Catherine, who ate most of her meals in bed. Do the laundry whenever it was needed. Dust, sweep, and shake rugs in every part of the house. Bake bread and desserts, while making sure that each meal was fixed on time.

Allison had to squeeze in a few minutes before bed at night in order to read her Bible. And she had been negligent about letter writing. She'd only written to Aaron twice, once to let him know she had arrived home safely, and another earlier this week to tell him how her aunt was doing and that she missed him. She'd also written to Aunt Mary and Uncle Ben. Aunt Mary had sent one letter in return, but Aaron had written several times, saying how much he missed Allison and that he was praying for her aunt. He also mentioned that Melinda had given birth to a baby boy last week and said he hoped Allison would return to Missouri soon so she could see the cute boppli.

Allison yawned and took a seat on the edge of her bed, planning to read a Bible passage before she fell asleep. *I don't want Aaron to get his hopes up about me going back there, because unless God provides a miracle, it doesn't look like Aunt Catherine will make it. If she dies, Papa will still need me here.*

As Allison read John 3:16 and reflected on how God had sent His only Son to die for the sins of the world, she felt a sense of urgency well up within her soul. She'd tried on several occasions to witness to her aunt, but every time she brought up the subject of heaven, Aunt Catherine either said she was tired and wanted to sleep, or she became irritable, often shouting at Allison to get out of her room.

"Dear Lord," Allison prayed, "please give me the opportunity to speak with Aunt Catherine about You soon, and I ask that You will open her heart to the Good News."

twenty-seven

By the first of November, Aunt Catherine had become so weak she spent most of her time in bed. The pain in her body had intensified, but she refused any medication. Allison knew if she was going to get through to her aunt with the message of salvation it would have to be soon. She'd tried several times to broach the subject, but her aunt always said she didn't want to talk about it, though she wouldn't say why. In desperation, Allison formulated a plan. She would make Aunt Catherine a faceless doll and attach a passage of scripture to it, the way Melinda's stepfather did with the desserts he baked to give to folks with a need. Maybe the verse would touch her aunt's heart in a way Allison couldn't do with words.

Allison headed for the treadle sewing machine, which she discovered was covered with dust. It had obviously been some time since it had been put to use. Carefully, she cut out a girl doll using the pattern Aunt Mary had given her. She also cut enough material to make a dark blue dress with a black cape and apron, a pair of black stockings, and a small white kapp. It made her think of the doll Mama had made—the one she'd left behind in Missouri because it was missing. Allison had clung to the doll during her growing-up years, and even though she missed it, she realized what she missed most was not an inanimate object, but people—her aunt, uncle, and cousins—and especially Aaron Zook.

Should I continue to write Aaron letters, or would it be better if I made a clean break? Allison continued to ponder the situation as she sewed the doll. Maybe she should wait until after Christmas to make a decision. Or would it be better to do it now, while it was fresh on her mind?

"The letter can wait awhile," she murmured as she slipped a

155

piece of muslin under the pressure foot of the treadle machine. "Right now, I need to concentrate on making this doll and deciding which verse of scripture to attach."

&

"What are you doin' over there?" Aaron asked his youngest sister, Emma, as he stepped into the barn and discovered her huddled in one corner near some bales of straw. Since he'd heard their mamm call Emma a few minutes ago, Aaron figured the child might have snuck off to the barn to play with the kittens when she should have been inside helping set the table for supper.

Emma jumped, like she'd been caught doing something bad, and she looked up at Aaron with both hands behind her back.

"What have you got that you don't want me to see?" he asked, taking a step closer.

She backed away, until her legs bumped a bale of straw. "Nothin'. Just girl stuff."

"What kind of girl stuff would you need to hide?"

She hung her head but gave no reply.

"Emma, hold your hands out so I can see."

Her shoulders trembled, and Aaron figured she was close to tears.

"If you've got something you're not supposed to have, then you'd better give it to me." Aaron's patience was beginning to wane.

"I—I didn't mean to keep it. I was only gonna borrow it, but then—"

"Borrow what, Emma?"

She sniffed, and when she looked up at Aaron, he noticed there were tears in her eyes. "I borrowed this—from Allison Troyer."

Aaron's mouth dropped open as Emma extended her hands, revealing a faceless doll with no kapp on its head. He knew immediately it was the one Allison's mother had given her when she was a young girl.

"Why, Emma? Why would you take something that wasn't yours?"

Her voice quavered when she spoke. "I–I've asked Mama to make me a doll, but she always says she's too busy takin' care of Grandma and Grandpa. I think she loves them more than she does me."

Aaron's heart went out to Emma even though he knew what she had done was wrong. He knelt in front of the little girl and gathered her into his arms. "If I had known you wanted a doll so badly, I would have asked Allison to make you one. She sews faceless dolls and has even sold some to the gift shop at the bed-and-breakfast in town."

Emma opened her mouth as if to say something, but he cut her off. "As far as our mamm lovin' her folks more than she does you, that's just plain silly. They have health problems, and she wants to care for them during their old age. But you're her little girl, and she loves you very much." He patted her gently on the back. "Remember when you were in the hospital because of your appendix?"

"Jah."

"Mama and Paul—uh—your daed, came to see you every day, and during the first twenty-four hours after your surgery they never left the hospital. Did you know that?"

She hiccupped on a sob. "Huh-uh."

"Do you think they would have done that if they didn't love you?"

"I guess not."

Aaron took the doll from his sister. "This isn't yours, and takin' it was wrong. You'll need to tell Mama what you've done."

Tears streamed down Emma's cheeks. "Do I have to, Aaron? What if she gives me a bletching?"

Aaron squeezed her shoulders gently. "I haven't known our mamm to give out too many spankings over the years, but I'm sure you'll receive whatever punishment she feels you deserve." He stood. "I'll see that this doll is sent to Allison, and I'll be sure and tell her how sorry you are for taking it."

She nodded. "Jah, please tell her that, for I surely wish I hadn't done it."

He pointed to the barn door. "Run into the house now and set things straight with Mama. I'll be in shortly."

Emma hesitated, gave Aaron a quick hug around his legs, and darted out the door.

Aaron stared at the bedraggled doll. "Allison will sure be surprised when I mail her this." He smiled. "Maybe I'll wait awhile and send it to her for Christmas."

❧

Allison crept quietly into her aunt's room, unsure if she would find her asleep or not.

The floor squeaked, and Aunt Catherine's eyes opened. Allison smiled, but her aunt only stared at her with a vacant look. *Doesn't she know who I am? How close might she be to dying?*

"Aunt Catherine, I brought you something," Allison said as she approached the bed.

No response.

"It's a faceless doll, and I made it myself." She held the doll in front of her aunt's face.

Aunt Catherine moaned, as though she were in terrible pain.

"Are you hurting real bad? Is there something I can get for you?"

"I—I've always wanted one."

"What do you want?"

"A faceless doll." Aunt Catherine lifted a shaky hand as tears gathered in the corner of her eyes.

Allison handed the doll to her aunt, and the woman clutched it to her chest with a trembling sob. "My mamm wouldn't allow dolls in the house when I was a girl—not even the faceless kind."

"I'm so sorry." Allison's throat clogged with tears. Through all the years Aunt Catherine had lived with them, she'd never thought about how things must have been for her aunt when she was a child. Allison knew Aunt Catherine had grown up with seven brothers and no sisters, but she didn't have any idea the poor woman had been denied the pleasure of owning a faceless doll. All these years Allison had only focused on how mean Aunt Catherine was and how she'd never felt that the woman cared for her. *Maybe if I'd shown love first, it would have been given in return,* she thought ruefully.

"Wh–what's this?" Aunt Catherine asked, touching the slip of paper pinned to the back of the doll's skirt.

"A verse of scripture," Allison replied. "It's one Aunt Mary quoted to me on the day I asked Jesus to forgive my sins. Would you like me to read it to you?"

Aunt Catherine's expression turned stony, and Allison feared she might throw the doll aside or yell at Allison to get out of the room. Instead, her aunt began to cry. First it came out in a soft whine, but then it turned to convulsing sobs. "I've sinned many times over the years." She drew in a raspy breath. "I'm going to die soon, and I don't think I'll make it to heaven. Oh, Allison, I'm so scared."

Aunt Catherine's confession was almost Allison's undoing. She took a seat on the edge of the bed and reached for her aunt's hand. "You can go to heaven, Aunt Catherine. The Bible says we have all sinned and come short of the glory of God. But He provided a way for us to get to heaven, through the blood of His Son, Jesus." She paused to gauge her aunt's reaction, but the woman said nothing, just lay there staring vacantly, like she had when Allison first came into the room.

"I used to feel faceless before God," Allison went on to say. "But I know I'm not faceless, because the Bible tells us in Jeremiah 29:13 that the Lord said we will seek Him and find Him when we search for Him with all our heart." She smiled. "After I accepted Jesus as my personal Savior, a sense of peace and purpose came over me. If I were to die today, I know my soul would enter into the place where my heavenly Father lives."

"Heaven," Aunt Catherine murmured, as if she were being drawn back into the conversation.

Allison nodded. "Romans 10:9 says, 'That if thou shalt confess with thy mouth the Lord Jesus, and shalt believe in thine heart that God hath raised him from the dead, thou shalt be saved.' Would you like me to pray with you, Aunt Catherine, so you can confess your sins and tell the Lord you believe in Him as your Savior?"

"Jah, I would."

Aunt Catherine closed her eyes and Allison did the same. Allison prayed the same prayer Aunt Mary had prayed with her, and Aunt Catherine repeated each word. When the prayer ended, a look of peace flooded the dying woman's face. Allison knew that no matter when the Lord chose to take Aunt Catherine home, she would go to heaven and spend eternity with Him.

twenty-eight

As Allison headed down the driveway toward their mailbox, she let her tears flow unchecked. Yesterday had been Aunt Catherine's funeral, and despite any negative feelings she'd had for her aunt in the past, Allison knew she would miss the woman. She and Aunt Catherine had been given the chance to make peace, and for that she felt grateful. Most of all, Allison felt joy that her aunt had accepted Christ as her Savior and now rested in His arms.

Allison thought about Aunt Catherine's final days on earth and the request she'd made one week before her death. "Peanut brittle. Let me taste some peanut brittle."

Even though her aunt had been too weak to chew the hard candy, Allison honored the appeal. Using the recipe she'd found tucked inside Aunt Catherine's cookbook, Allison had made a batch of peanut brittle.

She could still see the expression on her aunt's face when she had placed a small piece of it between her lips. "Umm. . .gut."

Allison knew that from that day on, whenever she ate peanut brittle, she would think of Aunt Catherine and the precious moments they'd spent together over the last few months.

Allison glanced at the letter in her hand. She had planned to wait until after Christmas to write Aaron and tell him she would be staying in Pennsylvania. But why prolong things? Wouldn't it be better if she made a clean break so Aaron could move on with his life? Now that Aunt Catherine was gone, Papa needed Allison more than ever. As much as it hurt to tell Aaron good-bye, she knew it would be best if he found someone else.

Allison opened the mailbox flap, placed the letter inside, and lifted the red flag. With tears blurring her vision, she turned toward the house. *This is for the best—jah, truly it is.*

๛

Aaron's hands trembled as he read the letter he had just received from Allison. She wasn't coming back to Webster County. Her aunt had died, and her father needed someone to cook and clean for him.

"Doesn't Allison know that I need her, too?" he mumbled. "I don't want to court anyone else. It's her I love."

Aaron thought about the faceless doll Allison's mother had made and how he'd discovered his sister had taken it. He had planned to send the doll to Allison for Christmas, but he wondered if it would be best to put it in the mail now and be done with it.

He sank to the stool behind his workbench and groaned. "It isn't fair."

"What's wrong, son? You look like you've lost your best friend," Paul said, moving across the room to stand beside Aaron.

"I have lost a friend." Aaron handed the letter to his step-father. "Allison's not comin' back to Missouri. Her aunt passed away, and she says her daed needs her there."

Paul frowned. "I'm sorry about her aunt—and sorry Allison won't be returning to Webster County." He placed his hand on Aaron's shoulder. "You care for her a lot, don't you, son?"

Aaron's only reply was a quick nod. There was no use denying it, but there wasn't much point in talking about it, either.

"From what I could tell when Allison was visiting for the summer, she was a lot like your mamm," Paul said.

"She's the kind of woman I've always wanted but never thought I would find." Aaron grunted. "Wish I'd never even met her."

Paul pulled another stool over beside Aaron and took a seat. "This isn't an impossible situation, you know."

"As far as I can tell, it is."

Paul shook his head. "Have you forgotten that I used to live in Lancaster County?"

"No, I haven't forgotten. I remember when you first came here for your brother's funeral and decided to stay on so you could help Mama in the harness shop."

"That's right. I thought I would only be here a few months—just until your mamm got her strength back after Davey was born. Then I figured I'd be on my way back to Pennsylvania, where I worked at my cousin's harness shop."

"But you ended up stayin' and marryin' Mama."

Paul nodded. "That's right. I loved that woman so much—and would have done about anything to marry her." He squeezed Aaron's shoulder. "I loved you and your brothers and still do."

Aaron's throat clogged and he swallowed hard.

"There is a way for you and Allison to be together, Aaron. You can move to Pennsylvania, and we can see if my cousin would be willing to hire you at his harness shop."

Aaron's mouth dropped open. "And leave you in the lurch? Mama's not able to help out here anymore, and there's too much work for one man."

Paul pursed his lips, as though in deep thought. "Guess I could see if Joseph or Zachary might want to work here. Neither one has shown any interest in the harness shop, so I'd have to train them, of course."

"What about Davey? Do you think he might want to be your apprentice?" Aaron asked, hope welling up in his chest.

"Might could be. Between the three boys, I'm sure one of 'em would agree to take your place so you can be with the woman you love."

Aaron blew out his breath. "You really think it could work?"

"Don't see why not." Paul patted Aaron on the back. "When there's love involved, there's gotta be a way."

"How soon would I be able to leave?"

"I think your mamm would be sorely disappointed if you weren't here for Christmas. How about right after the first of the year?"

Aaron nodded enthusiastically. "Sounds gut to me. I think

I won't send Allison's doll to her now. I'll take it with me when I go." He grinned and hopped off the stool. "I won't tell her I'm comin', either. Might be more fun to show up unannounced."

❧

For the next several weeks, Allison forced herself to act cheerful in front of Papa and Peter, but when she was alone in the house she allowed her grief to surface. Oh, how she missed Aaron and her family in Webster County. She missed making faceless dolls and spending time with Melinda and Katie. She even missed her cooking lessons and housekeeping chores. Of course, she had cooking and cleaning to do here, but it wasn't nearly as fun or rewarding as it had been under Aunt Mary's tutelage.

Allison stirred the pot of stew sitting on the back burner of their propane-operated stove and sighed. If only she could forget about Aaron. Truth was, she wished they'd never met because it was too painful to find love and then lose it.

The back door slammed shut and she jumped.

"Sorry. Didn't mean to frighten you," Papa said, brushing the snow off his woolen jacket.

"I didn't think you'd be in so soon. Supper won't be ready for another half hour or so."

"That's okay. I'm not hungry yet, anyway." He ambled over to the sink and turned on the faucet.

"Where's Peter?" Allison asked.

"He went over to Sally's house for supper again."

"So it's just the two of us?"

"Jah."

When Papa finished washing up, he took a seat at the kitchen table. "Why don't you turn down the burner and come have a seat? I have somethin' I want to give you." He motioned to the chair across from him.

Allison shrugged but did as he asked.

Papa reached into his shirt pocket and pulled out an envelope. "This is for you—an early Christmas present." He leaned across the table and handed it to her.

Allison tipped her head. "What is it? A letter?"

"Take a look."

She tore open the envelope, and her mouth fell open. Surely this couldn't be!

❧

Aaron held a piece of leather out to Zachary. "You didn't get it stained right, and now you'll have to do it over again."

Zachary's eyebrows drew together. "You're too picky, ya know that? I'll bet Pop will be easier to work with than you are."

"That's what you think." Aaron ruffled his brother's brown hair. "Paul knows the harness business well, and he expects only the best. So you'd better learn to listen if you're gonna work here after I leave for Pennsylvania."

Zachary leaned against the workbench. "Sure hate to see ya move." He glanced around and lowered his voice. "I would never admit this to Pop, but harness work ain't my first choice for an occupation."

"What would you rather be doin'?"

"Well, I've helped out at Osborn's Christmas Tree Farm some, and I've really enjoyed it."

Aaron's eyebrows drew together. "If you'd rather work there, then why'd you agree to take over for me?"

Zachary shrugged. "Pop said you're in love with Allison Troyer, and I didn't wanna be the one blamed for keepin' you two apart."

Aaron's heart sank clear to his toes. How could he take off for Pennsylvania knowing his brother was making such a sacrifice for him? Yet, how could he stay when he loved Allison and wanted to be with her?

The bell above the front door jingled, but he didn't bother to go up front to see who'd come in. Paul was working at his desk, which was near the door, so he could wait on the customer.

A few seconds later, Paul called, "Zachary, can I see you a minute?"

Zachary looked at Aaron and shrugged. "Guess I'd best go see what the boss wants, or I'll be in trouble."

Aaron went back to work on the bridle he was making for Ben King and tried not to think about Zachary's admission that he didn't really want to do harness work.

"Hello, Aaron."

Aaron looked up and his breath caught in his throat. "Allison? What are you doin' here?"

She took a few steps toward him. "I came to see you."

"But—I thought—I mean—I was going to—" Aaron knew he was stammering, but he seemed powerless to say anything intelligent right now. Allison looked so sweet, standing there smiling at him, and he just wanted to reach out and hug her.

"Papa gave me an early Christmas present—a one-way bus ticket to Webster County, Missouri." She smiled. "I'm hopin' to stay here for good this time."

Aaron's heartbeat picked up speed. "You—you are?"

She nodded. "If it's not too late for you and me, that is."

"I thought you had to stay in Pennsylvania to care for your daed." His brain felt fuzzy, like it was full of cotton.

"I thought so, too, but Peter's marrying Sally Mast soon, and they've agreed to move in with Papa. Peter thinks it will be easier for him to keep working at the dairy farm if he lives nearby, and Sally told me she's happy to take care of the house and do all the cooking."

Aaron could hardly contain himself. "Do you know what this means, Allison?"

"I think it means we can begin courting again—if you haven't found someone else, that is."

He shook his head and reached for her hand. "Never!"

"I'm glad."

"What this means is that I can stay right here and keep workin' for Paul in the harness shop. Fact is, I'd be happy to work here even if I never get to call the shop my own."

Allison tipped her head. "What do you mean?"

"I was planning to move to Pennsylvania so I could be near

you." He pulled her into his arms and drew in a deep breath, relishing the pleasant aroma of her clean-smelling hair. "I was going to show up at your door and surprise you right after the first of the year, but you've surprised me instead."

"You would have moved to Pennsylvania for me?"

"A man in love will do most anything for the woman he loves."

Allison's eyes welled up with tears. "You really love me?"

"Jah, I do. And I also have a special present for you." Aaron moved to the other side of the room and pulled a small cardboard box from one of the shelves. When he handed it to Allison, she gave him a questioning look.

"What's this?"

"Open it," he said with a smile.

She lifted the lid on the box and gasped. "My faceless doll! Oh, Aaron, where did you find it?"

"I'll explain that later. Right now, would you mind reading the note attached to the back of the doll?"

Allison turned the doll over and read the message written on a piece of paper that had been pinned to the doll's dress. *"Will you marry me, Allison Troyer?"*

Tears welled up in Allison's eyes and threatened to spill over. "You—really want me to be your wife?"

"Jah, if you're willing."

She nodded and gave in to her tears, allowing them to trickle down her cheeks. "Jah, I'll marry you, but there is one condition."

He squinted. "What might that be?"

"That I'm allowed to work here in the harness shop with you."

Aaron chuckled as relief flooded his soul. "Now that's a deal I can't refuse." He drew Allison into his arms and kissed her, thanking God for the way He had worked everything out. Aaron looked forward to spending the rest of his days on a journey of love with this special woman.

epilogue

two years later

Allison sat at the treadle sewing machine, humming softly as she sewed a faceless doll. She glanced across the room, where her one-year-old daughter, Catherine, sat on the floor, playing with the same doll Allison's mother had made many years ago.

Allison reached for the verse she planned to attach to the doll she was making. On each one she sewed, she included a passage of scripture: *"Ye shall seek me, and find me, when ye shall search for me with all your heart. . .saith the LORD." Jeremiah 29:13–14*

Aaron stepped into the kitchen and bent to kiss her. "How're my two favorite women?"

"We're doin' fine," Allison replied with a smile. "I was just sitting here thinking how my coming to Webster County has changed my life."

He swooped their daughter into his arms and took a seat in the rocking chair beside the stove. "Want to tell us how your life has changed?"

"If I hadn't come here and met my mamm's twin sister, I might never have found the Lord as my Savior." She lifted the pressure foot and pulled the doll free, holding it up for her husband's inspection. "And I would never have learned to make these faceless friends."

He nodded. "Anything else?"

Allison leaned over and reached for Aaron's hand, placing both of their hands on their little girl's head. "If I hadn't moved to Webster County, I wouldn't be married to the new owner of Zook's Harness Shop, or be the mama of this sweet little girl I love so much." She chuckled. "Course, I love Catherine's daed, too."

Aaron grinned. "Sure was a surprise when Paul—I mean, Pop, decided it was time to retire and turn the shop over to us, wasn't it?"

"The Lord is good, and nothing He does surprises me." Allison pointed to the doll nestled in little Catherine's arms. "I'm glad I no longer feel faceless before God, the way I did before I asked Jesus to forgive my sins." She smiled and blinked back the tears of joy that had clouded her vision. "No matter how long I'm allowed to journey this earth, I pray that I can share the joy of the Lord with everyone who receives one of my faceless friends."

RECIPE FOR AUNT CATHERINE'S PEANUT BRITTLE

Ingredients:

  2 cups sugar
  ½ cup water
  1 cup white Karo syrup
  1 tsp. vanilla
  2 tsp. baking soda
  3 cups raw peanuts
  1 tsp. butter

In a kettle over medium heat, cook the Karo syrup, sugar, and water to the hardball stage. Add butter and peanuts. Stir and cook until it just turns brown. Remove from stove. Add vanilla and soda. Spread over a large buttered cookie sheet and cool. Cut or break into pieces and serve.

author's note

It is written in the book of Deuteronomy that one should not produce any human images or likenesses. For this reason, the Amish don't allow their dolls to have faces, so they don't resemble human beings. In earlier years, even faceless dolls were forbidden. Due to this custom, some Amish children were given a piece of wood wrapped in a blanket to serve as their baby. Faceless dolls reflect the beliefs and traditions handed down from generation to generation.

A Letter To Our Readers

Dear Reader:
In order that we might better contribute to your reading enjoyment, we would appreciate your taking a few minutes to respond to the following questions. We welcome your comments and read each form and letter we receive. When completed, please return to the following:

Fiction Editor
Heartsong Presents
PO Box 719
Uhrichsville, Ohio 44683

1. Did you enjoy reading *Allison's Journey* by Wanda E. Brunstetter?
   ❑ Very much! I would like to see more books by this author!
   ❑ Moderately. I would have enjoyed it more if

   _____

   _____

   _____

2. Are you a member of **Heartsong Presents**? ❑ Yes ❑ No
   If no, where did you purchase this book? _____

   _____

3. How would you rate, on a scale from 1 (poor) to 5 (superior), the cover design? _____

4. On a scale from 1 (poor) to 10 (superior), please rate the following elements.

   ____ Heroine   ____ Plot
   ____ Hero   ____ Inspirational theme
   ____ Setting   ____ Secondary characters

5. These characters were special because? _____

_____

_____

6. How has this book inspired your life? _____

_____

_____

7. What settings would you like to see covered in future
   Heartsong Presents books? _____

_____

_____

8. What are some inspirational themes you would like to see
   treated in future books? _____

_____

_____

9. Would you be interested in reading other **Heartsong
   Presents** titles? ❏ Yes   ❏ No

10. Please check your age range:
    ❏ Under 18   ❏ 18-24
    ❏ 25-34   ❏ 35-45
    ❏ 46-55   ❏ Over 55

Name _____

Occupation _____

Address _____

City, State, Zip_____

fresh-brewed love

4 stories in 1

Four women find grounds for love where romance blossoms over cups of coffee. Can these women make the right decisions when it comes to love? Authors include Susan K. Downs, Anita Higman, DiAnn Mills, and Kathleen Y'Barbo.

Contemporary, paperback, 352 pages, 5³/₁₆" x 8"

Hearts♥ng

CONTEMPORARY ROMANCE IS CHEAPER BY THE DOZEN!

Buy any assortment of twelve *Heartsong Presents* **titles and save 25% off the already discounted price of $2.97 each!**

Any 12 Heartsong Presents titles for only $27.00*

*plus $2.00 shipping and handling per order and sales tax where applicable.

HEARTSONG PRESENTS TITLES AVAILABLE NOW:

___HP405 *The Wife Degree*, A. Ford
___HP406 *Almost Twins*, G. Sattler
___HP409 *A Living Soul*, H. Alexander
___HP410 *The Color of Love*, D. Mills
___HP413 *Remnant of Victory*, J. Odell
___HP414 *The Sea Beckons*, B. L. Etchison
___HP417 *From Russia with Love*, C. Coble
___HP418 *Yesteryear*, G. Brandt
___HP421 *Looking for a Miracle*, W. E. Brunstetter
___HP422 *Condo Mania*, M. G. Chapman
___HP425 *Mustering Courage*, L. A. Coleman
___HP426 *To the Extreme*, T. Davis
___HP429 *Love Ahoy*, C. Coble
___HP430 *Good Things Come*, J. A. Ryan
___HP433 *A Few Flowers*, G. Sattler
___HP434 *Family Circle*, J. L. Barton
___HP438 *Out in the Real World*, K. Paul
___HP441 *Cassidy's Charm*, D. Mills
___HP442 *Vision of Hope*, M. H. Flinkman
___HP445 *McMillian's Matchmakers*, G. Sattler
___HP449 *An Ostrich a Day*, N. J. Farrier
___HP450 *Love in Pursuit*, D. Mills
___HP454 *Grace in Action*, K. Billerbeck
___HP458 *The Candy Cane Calaboose*, J. Spaeth
___HP461 *Pride and Pumpernickel*, A. Ford
___HP462 *Secrets Within*, G. G. Martin
___HP465 *Talking for Two*, W. E. Brunstetter
___HP466 *Risa's Rainbow*, A. Boeshaar
___HP469 *Beacon of Truth*, P. Griffin
___HP470 *Carolina Pride*, T. Fowler
___HP473 *The Wedding's On*, G. Sattler
___HP474 *You Can't Buy Love*, K. Y'Barbo
___HP477 *Extreme Grace*, T. Davis
___HP478 *Plain and Fancy*, W. E. Brunstetter
___HP481 *Unexpected Delivery*, C. M. Hake
___HP482 *Hand Quilted with Love*, J. Livingston
___HP485 *Ring of Hope*, B. L. Etchison
___HP486 *The Hope Chest*, W. E. Brunstetter
___HP489 *Over Her Head*, G. G. Martin

___HP490 *A Class of Her Own*, J. Thompson
___HP493 *Her Home or Her Heart*, K. Elaine
___HP494 *Mended Wheels*, A. Bell & J. Sagal
___HP497 *Flames of Deceit*, R. Dow & A. Snaden
___HP498 *Charade*, P. Humphrey
___HP501 *The Thrill of the Hunt*, T. H. Murray
___HP502 *Whole in One*, A. Ford
___HP505 *Happily Ever After*, M. Panagiotopoulos
___HP506 *Cords of Love*, L. A. Coleman
___HP509 *His Christmas Angel*, G. Sattler
___HP510 *Past the Ps Please*, Y. Lehman
___HP513 *Licorice Kisses*, D. Mills
___HP514 *Roger's Return*, M. Davis
___HP517 *The Neighborly Thing to Do*, W. E. Brunstetter
___HP518 *For a Father's Love*, J. A. Grote
___HP521 *Be My Valentine*, J. Livingston
___HP522 *Angel's Roost*, J. Spaeth
___HP525 *Game of Pretend*, J. Odell
___HP526 *In Search of Love*, C. Lynxwiler
___HP529 *Major League Dad*, K. Y'Barbo
___HP530 *Joe's Diner*, G. Sattler
___HP533 *On a Clear Day*, Y. Lehman
___HP534 *Term of Love*, M. Pittman Crane
___HP537 *Close Enough to Perfect*, T. Fowler
___HP538 *A Storybook Finish*, L. Bliss
___HP541 *The Summer Girl*, A. Boeshaar
___HP542 *Clowning Around*, W. E. Brunstetter
___HP545 *Love Is Patient*, C. M. Hake
___HP546 *Love Is Kind*, J. Livingston
___HP549 *Patchwork and Politics*, C. Lynxwiler
___HP550 *Woodhaven Acres*, B. Etchison
___HP553 *Bay Island*, B. Loughner
___HP554 *A Donut a Day*, G. Sattler
___HP557 *If You Please*, T. Davis
___HP558 *A Fairy Tale Romance*, M. Panagiotopoulos
___HP561 *Ton's Vow*, K. Cornelius
___HP562 *Family Ties*, J. L. Barton

(If ordering from this page, please remember to include it with the order form.)

Presents

Great Inspirational Romance at a Great Price!

Heartsong Presents books are inspirational romances in contemporary and historical settings, designed to give you an enjoyable, spirit-lifting reading experience. You can choose wonderfully written titles from some of today's best authors like Andrea Boeshaar, Wanda E. Brunstetter, Yvonne Lehman, Joyce Livingston, and many others.

When ordering quantities less than twelve, above titles are $2.97 each.
Not all titles may be available at time of order.

SEND TO: **Heartsong Presents** Readers' Service
P.O. Box 721, Uhrichsville, Ohio 44683

Please send me the items checked above. I am enclosing $ _____
(please add $2.00 to cover postage per order. OH add 7% tax. NJ
add 6%). Send check or money order, no cash or C.O.D.s, please.
To place a credit card order, call 1-740-922-7280.

NAME _____

ADDRESS _____

CITY/STATE _____ ZIP_____

HP 1-06